THE RED

SUITCASE

SUSAN

BURROWS

For Barbara June Burrows

CHAPTER ONE
Australia
1953

It was a typical warm summer morning as the sun peeked over the rolling hills on the outskirts of Perth, Western Australia. As the two sisters drove the old family truck into town, they were so relieved about being away from home, they did not really care if Elizabeth won the ribbon or not. The local beauty pageants were more coming-out events for young women in Australia. This was Elizabeth's fourth event, and she had won or come in second place at all of them. Her younger sister, Abby, was always by her side as companion and chaperone, and they were both happy to get away from the watchful eye of Mother Merrick. Although Elizabeth didn't say anything to Abby, something inside her was telling her this pageant was going to be different. As she drove the truck over the winding and dusty roads, she sensed her life was about to change. As they continued driving west toward Perth, they were both full of apprehension. Elizabeth worried how she would keep an eye on Abby, but was mostly afraid Abby would do something to embarrass her. Even so, she couldn't imagine Abby not being with her and was truly thankful her little sister was sitting beside her, especially since their parents did not approve of these pageants. Both girls had made such a fuss about attending the Miss Western Australia Pageant in Perth, the largest pageant Elizabeth had ever entered, they finally gave in and let Elizabeth send in her photos and questionnaire. They were not surprised when she was accepted, but were more concerned she might actually win this one, and they were nervous about the publicity and exposure Elizabeth might encounter.

Abby sat silently watching the road, knowing if she didn't Elizabeth would miss the turnoff for downtown Perth. She loved Elizabeth and thought she was the most beautiful girl in all of Western Australia—and possibly all of Australia. Elizabeth's long, dark hair and blue eyes, combined with her long legs and shapely figure, made Abby wish she looked more like her sister. She knew she was going to be pretty, but not like her big sister. Elizabeth was graceful and intelligent, and there was always a stream of young men who wanted to court her. But they scared Elizabeth. She didn't want to be trapped in Boora Rock, Australia. She wanted to travel, meet interesting people, and go to college. The last thing Elizabeth Merrick wanted was to settle down in Boora Rock, like her mother had, and she let everyone know exactly how she felt. Abby knew this all too well about her sister, and planned to follow right along with her.

They eventually came to the turn to downtown Perth, and as Abby expected, Elizabeth missed the turn and they had to double back. As they drove down Main Street, they noticed the parking spaces were all taken and the sidewalks were full of people who were very dressed up. The men wore suits, while the women donned the prettiest summer dresses with matching bags and shoes. They were really surprised to see a NO VACANCY sign when they came to the luxurious Royal Hotel, that rarely happened as a result of their steep rates. A banner that read "Miss Western Australia 1953" was being hung above Main

Street, connecting the top corner of the First Western Australia Bank to the top corner of the courthouse building. As Elizabeth glanced at her little sister, she noticed her eyes were wide and transfixed as she took in the exciting bustle of the city. Elizabeth felt a knot growing in her stomach and wondered why she had ever entered the contest. She was certain she would lose and have to return home to face her mother telling her "I told you so" for years to come. She was even more frustrated now because she couldn't find a place to park the truck.

The lobby of the Royal Hotel was full of pageant contestants with their families, reporters, and promoters of the pageant, all vying for the best rooms. Several events were planned around the pageant that weekend, including cricket matches, a charity bake sale, and a fashion show. *Life* magazine was on hand, as well as representatives from the press associations from London to New York. Celebrities representing the promoters were making grand entrances into the lobby as some of the contestants took photographs and requested autographs. A particularly handsome young man entered the lobby, and the young pageant contestants clamored for an autograph and photo.

Elizabeth and Abby found a place to park the truck near the railroad station and began walking the five blocks carrying their heavy suitcases to the Saver Suites, located on the corner of Main and First Avenue, directly across the street from the Royal Hotel where the pageant was being held. It certainly was not as elegant as the Royal Hotel, but it was the best Mom and Dad could afford, and it was neat and clean. It also helped to assure the Merrick's their girls would be watched over. They knew the Powell's, who owned the Saver Suites, and they had promised to keep an eye on the girls.

Lunch for the pageant contestant would be served over at the Royal Hotel, with interviews to follow. Last-minute instructions were provided regarding the required clothing, proper posture, walking techniques, where to look, and when to smile. Elizabeth had a headache, but Abby was in awe.

CHAPTER TWO

A group of cricket players were gathered in the lobby for last-minute instructions and schedules for the weekend. Rex Stewart looked around him and noticed the best players of South Africa and Australia had been invited to play in this match. Joseph Davids and Albert Martin were there, and Rex knew he would enjoy playing with Joseph Davids, but was not looking forward to more of Albert Martin's annoying jokes and pranks.

As Rex partially listened to the information being provided by the team captain, he looked out the glass doors of the hotel lobby, across the street, to the entrance of the Saver Suites. He watched closely as a tall, beautiful girl with long legs struggled with an old and well-traveled red suitcase and a younger, shorter girl wrestled with another suitcase behind her. His eyes followed them until they disappeared into the lobby of the Saver Suites.

The Powell's gave the two sisters a warm welcome and asked about their trip. After they all exchanged embraces, Mr. Powell helped them carry their luggage to their room. It was one of the smaller rooms in the hotel, but clean and airy, with two beds and a very small dresser for their clothes. The two sisters immediately unpacked, and by noon Elizabeth had walked over to the Royal Hotel to get her schedule for the weekend activities.

The first event scheduled for 6:30 p.m. that evening in Ballroom Two was a fashion show, during dinner, featuring the pageant contestants as models. It was intended as part of the entertainment for families, the press, cricket players, and other attendees. It was also the contestants' formal introduction to the press and a first glimpse of the girls for the judges. The second event was on Saturday morning, a breakfast sale in the lobby of the Royal Hotel. There were not many restaurants in Perth open for breakfast and the Royal Hotel dining room could not accommodate everyone in town for the event. The Perth Ladies Club was donating coffee and tea, baked breakfast rolls, scones, and sweet cakes for the contestants to sell to the media, cricket players, and hotel guests. All proceeds from the breakfast sale would be donated to Perth's St. Cecilia's Orphanage. Elizabeth was assigned to one of the sweet cakes tables and was delighted when they told her Abby could help in the kitchen. Elizabeth wanted to keep Abby close by to be sure she stayed out of trouble. The next events were the swimsuit and evening gown portion, along with questions for the top finalists and a talent contest was scheduled for Saturday evening from 7:30 to 9:30 p.m. in the Royal Hotel Grand Ballroom. And, finally on Sunday, the crowned Miss Western Australia and the other top four winners would attend the final cricket match in the box seats of the WACA (Western Australia Cricket Association) grounds.

Elizabeth was most nervous about the question portion of the pageant. As far as the swimsuit and evening gown competition, she simply felt comfortable and confident in them, and she had decided long ago there was nothing she could do to change her figure. She was always self-conscious of her long legs, but now they seemed to be helping carry her out of Boora Rock.

She had no idea what questions would be asked and was worried they might ask questions about her family and hometown. She dreaded the idea of everyone knowing about Uncle Bill always having beer kegs open and the whole family, with the exception of her parents, getting louder and louder as they drank more beer. Usually she would hide in a quiet corner and read as soon as the beer keg was rolled out. This was the first pageant she had been in that had a question-and-answer portion, and she was relieved to hear there would be only one question for each contestant. Fortunately, due to the lack of anything the least bit interesting in Boora Rock, she spent a lot of time at the library and would read anything she could get her hands on. One of the teachers at her school, Miss Buck, had taken a special interest in Elizabeth and loaned her books from her personal collection, which was quite extensive. She would also let Elizabeth listen to all of her classical records anytime time she wanted. Elizabeth had done both every day since she was eight, so she hoped she would get a question pertaining to literature or music, her two favorite hobbies.

Friday afternoon, as the models were being fitted for the fashion show, the energy and excitement was boundless. However, Elizabeth was furious. She had been shown a picture of a little red cocktail dress she was to model in the show. *Red, of all colors!*, Elizabeth thought to herself. Even though the show featured fall collections, Elizabeth wanted a simple, basic look, which she felt suited her best. The dress was red and short, which would show more of her legs than she preferred, low-cut, and gathered snugly at the waist with an A-line skirt. Thanks to Mother Merrick's constant admonitions, Elizabeth believed she would be viewed negatively if she wore this dress.

During the fittings, the seamstress took pity on Elizabeth's horror and took a risk in changing the dress. With Elizabeth's direction, she changed the dress so it wasn't so gathered at the shoulders and let the material out so it produced a nice, simple round neckline that was not as low-cut. She did not hem the dress as short as the picture suggested, but just below Elizabeth's knee, giving her a long, sleek look that took advantage of her beautiful legs. When they were finished, the two of them felt they had created a stylish and elegant cocktail dress. The seamstress added a basic white pearl necklace and earrings to soften the look and presented Elizabeth with a pair of open-toed red heels.

The pageant consisted of fifteen contestants from every corner and small town in Western Australia. Each of the fifteen girls was provided a cocktail dress to model for the fashion show, to take place during a lavish dinner for the attendees. Tables for the event were arranged in a rectangular shape, with judges on the end and the guests seated at either long side. Each contestant had to enter, walk down the long path this configuration created and turn at the end, near the judges, and walk back. Elizabeth was upset again when she learned she had been chosen to go last. Everything about the pageant so far was not going well at all.

Back in her room at the Saver Suites, where Elizabeth had time to eat, shower, and dress before the fashion show started, Abby was chattering away about the celebrities and cricket players who were in attendance.

"Joseph Davids, Albert Martin, and a newcomer, Rex Stewart, who is apparently breaking wicket records and upsetting some of the seasoned players," she told Elizabeth.

"Abby, please! Do you have to go on? I just need to relax a little before the fashion show," Elizabeth said.

"But Elizabeth, they are all so tall and tanned and have the neatest-looking silk suits. Can't we meet some of them, or at least get a few autographs?"

Elizabeth was tired and was trying to think of something to say to discourage her sister from making any sort of scene. "Abby, you never listen to or watch the cricket matches. How is it you know so much about the game now?"

Unfortunately, Abby gushed excitedly "Well, I've been talking to all the kitchen help, and the maids here at the hotel, and all their brothers and fathers, just love cricket. Everyone is very excited about seeing Rex Stewart play. Can't we please get his autograph? Can't we, please?"

"Good God, Abby! We are not here to get autographs from the cricket players. And besides, Mom and Dad would have a fit if they knew what you've been up to." And, Elizabeth thought to herself, she didn't want Abby talking to the hotel help during the entire pageant. That would not help her image at all. Elizabeth finished the sandwich that Mrs. Powell had sent up for her, along with some fresh fruit, and headed for a bath. She hoped when she came out Abby wouldn't mention autographs again. Abby did not, as she had fallen asleep reading a *Life* magazine. Elizabeth left her a note telling her not to leave the room—she would be back in three hours.

The men from the cricket teams and the media were again gathered in the lobby of the Royal Hotel, in the bar area, where cigars and cocktails were being enjoyed in abundance. Their heads turned as they watched a file of pretty young women walk through the lobby and enter a side door, which appeared to connect to one of the main ballrooms. Rex Stewart noticed the tall, dark-haired girl he had spotted earlier, who was not smiling and seemed very nervous. Out of curiosity, he grabbed some of his teammates and led them to the ballroom, entering like any invited guest. They took a few empty seats in the back of the room, away from the rectangular-shaped area, and ordered more drinks from the waitress. They were still smoking their cigars and carrying on, their boisterous banter provoking raised eyebrows from the other guests already gathered in the room. They were cricket players, so no one made an issue of it.

Elizabeth, standing at the back of the line, watched in horror as the first girl came back from the stage in tears. Apparently, there were some loud and rowdy cricket players in the back of the room who had decided to attend the show and who whistled as she had made her walk. This made her so nervous; she slipped and fell into one of the judge's tables, spilling his tea. As time came closer for Elizabeth to take her turn, she watched more of the girls come back frustrated or crying and was glad now that she was last. She was also annoyed at these weak women who were letting a bunch of drunken cricket players ruin their chances of winning. She'd seen enough drunken men in Boora Rock to know better than to let them get to her.

By the time it was Elizabeth's turn, she was so angry and determined not to let those drunks in the back ruin her chances of getting out of Boora Rock, she threw back her shoulders, held her head high, and walked out. She could hear someone say in a slurred voice, "Hey, we want to see the swimsuits," and heard another whistle, but she was determined. When she reached the end of the rectangle, she looked directly at the cricket players, gave them a very confident smile, and winked at them. She turned and glided back, remembering to smile, head high and shoulders back, and most importantly, not to lose her footing. The minute she winked and turned, the room went silent. The men were so stunned they were speechless—for about five seconds. By the time she disappeared backstage, they were applauding and whistling like crazy, and they even stood up. Her boldness had paid off, as Elizabeth was voted best dressed and best poised.

That night, as the cricket players cavorted around the lobby bar, Rex couldn't get Elizabeth out of his mind. He knew her name now and that she was from Boora Rock. He had been there and knew there wasn't much to the small town. He guessed the other girl with the suitcase the day he'd first seen her was a relative. He was impressed that a girl from a small backwoods town had the gumption to walk up to his rowdy, drunken teammates and taunt them, especially seeing how nervous she had been when she'd first entered that room. He was definitely impressed, but quickly forgot about Elizabeth as he leaned down and kissed the busty blonde named Sarah who had been throwing herself at him all evening.

Back in her room at the Saver Suites with Abby, Elizabeth lay in bed, remembering the tall cricket player with the dark hair. When she peeked out the curtain after her walk, she saw him stand and applaud. One of the other girls, Sarah, who was blonde and had the largest bosom

Elizabeth had ever seen, told her his name was Rex Stewart. As she thought about her exciting day, Elizabeth realized she needed to stay focused and was worried about her most serious competition, Sarah.

Mrs. Powell, a large Irish woman who smelled like vanilla and was always smiling, came to check on the Merrick girls as she had promised their parents she would.

"How is it going? Are you two having fun?"

Abby had answered first, as usual. "Oh my gosh, there are so many people here, cricket players and reporters, and I think I even saw a movie star!"

"Yes, the town has been filled up for over a week, not a room to be had anywhere." She chuckled. "You're mighty quiet, Miss Elizabeth. Is everything all right?"

"Yes, it's just that the last event was made ever more difficult by a bunch of intoxicated cricket players who decided to crash the fashion show," Elizabeth said.

"Oh, well, don't let them get you too upset. They are just a bunch of young men who were simply trying to have some fun." She chuckled again. "Now you girls let me know if you need anything at all." She closed their door and left. Elizabeth could smell vanilla as Mrs. Powell walked down the hall.

After a good night's sleep, Elizabeth was feeling refreshed and energized. Up at 6:00 a.m., she and Abby were dressed, had eaten some of the biscuits their mother had packed, and had ordered a pot of tea. Abby was still pestering Elizabeth to get autographs, especially from the newcomer, Rex Stewart. They were at the Royal Hotel at seven thirty, and Abby headed to help in the kitchen as Elizabeth took her post at the sweet cakes table.

As she was organizing her table and getting ready for the breakfast crowd, she looked up and straight into the striking blue eyes of Rex Stewart as he asked for a piece of chocolate cake.

"Congratulations on your victory last night. You truly were the best dressed and the most beautiful," he said with a wide smile.

"Oh, well, thank you," Elizabeth answered, a little flustered. "Although if it weren't for you fellows making the other girls so nervous, I might not have won that portion of the contest," she said, wanting to let him know they had upset the contestants.

She handed him a slice of cake, and as he took it from her hand, he said, "I very much doubt that. I take it we did not make you nervous, Miss Merrick."

Elizabeth thought she saw a smile just before he devoured a huge chunk of the chocolate cake. She was surprised he remembered her name, but she did remember how angry his group had made her feel, and she said, "Nervous, no. I was actually very irritated."

As he paid her and set his plate down, he said, "I'm very sorry about all that. The guys are on the road so much they tend to get a little carried away. My sincerest apologies, and please pass them on to the other young ladies. Might I make it up to you by taking you to brunch when you are finished here?"

Just then, Abby came out of the kitchen with a platter of scones for the table next to Elizabeth's. She thought Abby might drop the platter when she saw Rex

19

Stewart talking to her. As she feared, Abby was headed directly for them.

Quickly she answered, "I'm sorry, but I'm here with my little sister."

"Not a problem," said Rex. "I would be delighted to escort two lovely ladies from Boora Rock to brunch. I'll be back at ten thirty to fetch you."

Before Elizabeth could reply, he was gone.

Rex was pleased with himself because he had not given her time to turn him down. He was accustomed to persuading the pretty girls to go out with him, but this was the first time he ever invited a younger sibling to go along. What was he thinking! He had a busy schedule this weekend—cricket at one thirty, and, hopefully, he would finish with the second match on Sunday. He was eager to beat Joseph Davids's scores, which would place him as the highest-ranking South African bowler to date. He knew he would have to stay focused in order to beat Joseph Davids, but he also knew that would be even more difficult now that he had met Elizabeth.

Back in their hotel room, Abby was talking nonstop about having brunch with Rex Stewart. "Could we have lots of photos taken and get his autograph? He's so handsome and tall, and everyone back home will be so jealous."

Elizabeth spent the next thirty minutes instructing Abby on what she should not discuss at brunch, even threatening to leave her behind and cancel altogether if she did not cooperate. The rules were simple: no talking about the family or Boora Rock in too much detail, and she was to follow Elizabeth's lead in the conversations.

After much anxiety over what they would wear to brunch, they headed back to the Royal Hotel. Rex greeted them, took each by an arm, and led them to a table on the veranda overlooking the gardens of the hotel. It was a beautiful scene, with a stone patio, and tables set with white linens and sky blue umbrellas. They overlooked the lawns, which also had tables with white linens and blue umbrellas scattered about and were accompanied by blue-and-white lounge chairs. Flowers were everywhere, of all different colors and varieties, surrounding two large marble fountains. It was so beautiful Elizabeth sat back in her chair and took a deep breath—until she saw Rex staring at her.

Fortunately, the waiter appeared at that moment to take their order. He spoke to Elizabeth first, but she asked him to start with Rex, who quickly ordered a coffee and a Coca-Cola, eggs, bacon, sausages, and pancakes. Abby, for some strange reason, copied Rex's order exactly. Elizabeth was famished, but remembered that evening was the swimsuits and evening gowns, so she ordered coffee and fresh fruit.

For a moment there was an awkward silence, until Rex asked Abby how she was keeping herself busy while Elizabeth was working the pageant. As they had rehearsed, she told him how Elizabeth had made arrangements for her to help out behind the scenes, but then she quickly launched into a barrage of questions, like how long had he been playing cricket, who was his hero, where was he born, and how old was he? Elizabeth was grateful for Abby at that moment and watched as Rex answered every question, starting with the latter, with a good-natured smile.

He was twenty-seven years old, he was born in Durban, South Africa, and his cricket hero was Dudley Nourse. When it came to answering how long he had been playing cricket, Elizabeth noticed his eyes light up, and she could see the passion he had for the game as he talked about how he started as a young boy with his two younger brothers, Robert and Colin, who played cricket as well. He started playing cricket on the Durban High School cricket team, and before he was out of high school, the clubs were asking him to play for them, and so his career as an international cricket player had begun.

Before Abby could launch into another line of questions, he turned to Elizabeth and said, "Enough of me for now. Elizabeth, I've actually been to Boora Rock, and there isn't much to the place, is there?"

"That's very true, and I'm anxious to leave as soon as possible. There is so much in this world that I want to see," she said.

"Yes, I know the feeling. However, I loved growing up in Durban because there was so much for me and my brothers to do. We were close to the beach and always ready to go on safari if we could get someone to take us. So, where do you think you would like to travel to first?"

The waiter brought the food, and fortunately, Abby dug right in. Elizabeth was pensive for a moment and replied, "Italy, I think, but I really would take anything compared to Boora Rock."

They both chuckled at that, and they spent the next hour talking mostly about Rex's travels through his cricket playing, which had taken him all over South Africa, Australia, and England. Elizabeth was fascinated, but wasn't sure he was as happy about his travels as he was about his cricket.

Rex looked at his watch and realized time had gone by quickly and he had to meet his teammates to prepare for the game. He asked Elizabeth and Abby if they would like to attend, and Abby piped in, "Oh yes, we would love to go. Can we Elizabeth, please?"

Knowing she had to prepare for the evening's competitions, she said they could go for a bit, but would have to leave early.

"Splendid," Rex said, "I will have someone save you a seat. I'm afraid I have to leave you ladies as I am late for a team meeting. Please stay as long as you like. I will see you both a little later" he thanked them for joining him at brunch and then he was gone.

As Elizabeth and Abby entered the Saver Suites, they saw Mrs. Powell dusting the small lobby area. She stopped to ask them how the bake sale had gone. "I hope you girls were able to sell a good amount to help those poor children at the orphanage."

"Yes," Elizabeth said, "it went quite well, and we were just having a late breakfast, as we were famished."

"Well, it must have been—look at the time!" Mrs. Powell said.

Abby was so excited about their date, she started to say, "We were having breakfast with—" when Elizabeth glared at her. She didn't want her parents pulling her out of the pageant, and they would if they knew she had taken Abby to brunch with a stranger.

Elizabeth offered, "We were just having a bite to eat with some people we met from the pageant." She hated lying, but she didn't want Mrs. Powell calling her parents.

"Well good, dear," Mrs. Powell replied. "It's good for you to have the opportunity to meet new people. Back to work for me." She scurried off to the lobby desk to greet a young couple who had just entered the lobby.

Mrs. Powell knew Elizabeth had lied to her as she had received a call from the hostess at the Royal Hotel who was a good friend of hers. She told her she had seen the girls with Rex Stewart. She had known for years about Elizabeth's desire to leave Boora Rock and frankly didn't blame her. There was nothing for young girls in that town. And she thought to herself, *Who knows, maybe this handsome cricket player will help her leave Boora Rock?* She was all for it. She would have to keep an eye on the two of them, though, as she had promised her parents she would.

"Welcome to the Saver Suites," Mrs. Powell chirped to the guests as she worked her way back to the reception desk.

Rex Stewart had quickly changed and was headed to the field. He was full from the large breakfast he had eaten. He must have been nervous, as he normally only had a candy bar for breakfast, and he didn't even remember inhaling all that food. He did remember how easy Elizabeth was to talk to. She seemed genuinely interested in his cricket career. She was so beautiful, and smart, and that was something different for him, as he was not usually attracted to the intellectual type. He couldn't figure out what it was about Elizabeth that had him thinking so much about her.

Later that day, at 7:00 p.m., Elizabeth was standing in her swimsuit next to Sarah, thinking about the handsome Rex Stewart. She and Abby had enjoyed watching him bowl that afternoon. He was very controlled and daring on the field, and she had not realized how popular he was. She thought he was easy to talk to although she had noticed, and was relieved, that he didn't ask her more questions about her background and family.

Just then Sarah said, "Are you coming to the party later tonight? Some of the cricket players are meeting in the lobby and invited me."

Elizabeth was surprised Rex hadn't invited her and wondered if he was the one who had invited Sarah. She didn't bother to reply. In fact, she pretended she hadn't heard her.

As she had expected she lost the swimsuit contest to, of course, Sarah. Elizabeth had to admit Sarah looked really good in her swimsuit, although she thought it was too low-cut and made her appear too busty. Elizabeth was changing into the evening gown she had brought with her for the next segment of the competition. It was a beautiful gold silk gown with long sleeves and high shoulders, V-necked, floor-length, and tapered at her feet. She also had matching gold high-heeled shoes and glistening earrings, and she knew she looked fantastic. She took great pride in this gown, as she had worked for six months to be able to afford the material and had designed and made it herself. While she was getting ready for her return to the stage, she was worried about the question-and-answer session, but first she had to make it to the final selections.

As she made her way down the runway in her gown, the applause erupted before she reached the end to make her turn. She noticed Rex and some of his teammates were again seated near the back of the room behind the judges, but this time they were behaving themselves. As she finished, the master of ceremonies announced it was time for the first cut—out of fifteen, ten would be eliminated now. Elizabeth had to admit she had heard the applause for Sarah when she made her walk too. She was getting nervous and told herself to remember to smile, and not let them see the nervousness on her face. After a few minutes of feeling uncomfortable and tense, the first ten were eliminated. Elizabeth was safe for now, and so was Sarah.

The mayor, acting as master of ceremonies of the pageant, asked the final five contestants to line up near him onstage to begin the question-and-answer session. First picked was Joann, the redheaded girl who was tall and had beautiful green eyes. Her question was regarding world history.

"Joann," the mayor said, "In what year did Matthew Flinders complete the first voyage around Australia?"

Joann was a bright girl, and this question should not be too difficult for anyone who graduated high school, Elizabeth thought.

She answered correctly. "In 1803, on the *Investigator*."

Two more contestants answered their questions, another of which was on a date in world history. To Elizabeth's amazement, the contestant answered incorrectly. She missed it by one year. Elizabeth's stomach was churning. Sarah was next and her question pertained to the United States.

"Who is the current president of the United States?"

Elizabeth could actually see Sarah breathe a sigh of relief as her bulging bosom rose and fell. She almost yelled the answer, "Harry Truman!"

"Yes, that is correct," the mayor said and asked her to step back in line. "Elizabeth Merrick, please approach the microphone." Elizabeth glided over with her golden silk dress flowing, hoping the microphone would not pick up the gurgling from her stomach. To her relief she was asked, "In what year was Henry Lawson's poem 'A Song of the Republic' first published?"

Thank God, Elizabeth thought to herself, a question on literature. She knew the answer before the mayor finished posing the question. She was very aware all eyes were on her, and she didn't want to react the way Sarah just had, so she carefully thought for a moment, looked at the audience, and answered, "It was first published in 1887," with a bright smile on her face.

"That is correct," the mayor said, and the audience applauded enthusiastically.

I made it, she said to herself as she walked back to her place with the other girls. The competition was down to her, Sarah, Joann, and one other girl named Olivia who Elizabeth did not know very well. She thought she was attractive, but Olivia's voice was so squeaky and annoying, she couldn't see her winning despite her good looks and intelligence.

The next portion of the pageant was the talent competition. The expectations for the winner were to be beautiful, graceful, intelligent, and talented. The girls changed from their gowns into their costumes, if required, and after an ear-piercing song by Olivia, and Joann's unfortunate fall during her tap dancing, they were both eliminated. It was down to just Sarah and Elizabeth; one would be crowned, and the other would be the runner-up to take the winner's place in case the winner could not perform her obligations as Miss Western Australia. Sarah sang a popular love song, slightly off-key, and Elizabeth had decided to do a jazz dance routine with black tights, a top hat, and cane. Her act went off without any problems, and she was very pleased and actually had fun. The audience applauded greatly, and she saw Rex and his friends standing and whistling in the back.

CHAPTER THREE

Elizabeth had won the Miss Western Australia title, Rex thought to himself. Not that he had had any doubt she would. He wanted to see her that night and celebrate and show her off to the team, but he had already asked Sarah to join him that evening. His career was on the rise and he was well aware of it. He wanted to be seen in public with the winner of the pageant, not a runner up, and was glad it turned out to be Elizabeth. He decided to talk to his teammate Rodney about Sarah. He knew she would be upset about being runner up and clinging to one of the South African cricket players. He wanted to make sure it wasn't him, so he talked with Rodney and assured him she was very pretty and would be great fun. Rex remembered kissing Sarah and how eager she had been to please him the night he'd brought her back to his hotel room. Yes, Rodney would be glad to be there to comfort Sarah this night.

Cameras were flashing away as Elizabeth accepted her check and crown, cradling an enormous bouquet of red long-stemmed roses as she took her final walk onstage. She was happy when she looked out at Abby and Mrs. Powell (whom she was surprised to see in the audience) and Rex. But more than happy she was relieved it was over. Between the stress of the events surrounding the pageant, all the wardrobe changes, and remembering to smile, stand straight, and be aware of her every move and action, she was completely drained. Her huge smile was from relief and also seeing Rex Stewart look up at her and mouth the words, "I'll meet you backstage."

When Elizabeth went backstage, she was greeted by all the other contestants, mostly offering insincere congratulations, with the exception of Joann. Standing behind them were Abby, Mrs. Powell, and Rex.

"You have to let me buy you a glass of champagne to celebrate," Rex said to her cheerfully.

"Oh, I don't know how we can; I have my sister to…" Elizabeth started to say, when to her surprise, Mrs. Powell spoke up.

"Oh, nonsense, Abby can come back to the hotel with me, and she will be just fine. You go on along with this nice Mr. Stewart and the rest of the girls to celebrate. Go on now."

"Splendid," Rex said. "I'll give you a few minutes to change."

Elizabeth was overwhelmed as she kissed Abby and Mrs. Powell and said good night to them. Just then the seamstress came in and gave Elizabeth the red cocktail dress she wore and told her to keep it.

"No one else can do it justice anyway," she said.

Elizabeth thanked her and quickly changed into the dress and shoes the seamstress had also given her, and hurried off to meet Rex. He kissed her on the cheek, put out his arm for her, and proudly escorted her into the lobby bar of the Royal Hotel.

Flashes from the photographers' cameras sparkled like stars in the night sky as they went wild taking pictures of the beauty queen and the new cricket sensation. They were a handsome couple, Rex thought to himself as he looked into Elizabeth's eyes just when the photographer snapped another picture.

Elizabeth drank her champagne and it did seem to calm her. She was still reeling from having won and thrilled that Rex was sitting right beside her. The photographers had all gone now, or at least put down their cameras and were enjoying themselves at the bar. "I knew you were going to win," Rex said as he sipped his scotch on the rocks.

Elizabeth replied, "Oh, I wasn't so sure at all, but I have to admit winning feels wonderful!"

Rex smiled and raised his glass to toast hers. "There is something about you, Elizabeth Merrick, that seems quite different from other girls I've met, and I can't figure out what it is."

"Well, I'm just like everyone else," she said and hoped he believed her. That is what she wanted at that moment—to be just like everyone else instead of an attractive girl who had just won a beauty pageant in hopes of leaving Boora Rock as soon as possible.

37

The band started to play a slow tune by Nat King Cole, and Rex took Elizabeth by the hand and led her onto the dance floor. They were a stunning, tall, dark couple, each with beautiful blue eyes, and they moved like they had been dancing together for years. Rex pulled Elizabeth close to him and breathed deeply, inhaling her scent and feeling her soft skin. The music ended, and they started to play a tango, and Elizabeth looked at him to see if he wanted to continue. He took her hand, and they launched right into the beat with all the drama and flair the music created. Everyone else stepped back as they danced, and just as Rex pulled her back into him after a double spin, Elizabeth thought she saw a camera flash.

Rodney spent most of the evening listening to Sarah's complaints about the pageant being unfair and how much she hated to go back home as he plied her with gin and tonics. He was surprised how much she could drink for a nineteen-year-old girl. She'd been crying, and her eye makeup was forming dark circles under her eyes, but she was a pretty girl and was wearing an extremely low-cut dress.

She allowed him to comfort her by first patting her on the back as he said, "It will be fine. There are other pageants to come around, and now you have time to prepare, not to worry." His pats turned into little hugs as his hand slipped to her side. She didn't seem to mind and, in fact, slid closer to him on her chair. She looked at him with her big brown eyes, like so many before her had, as he leaned in to kiss her. She readily kissed him back, and he knew it was time to take her back to his room. *Oh, how I love the game of cricket,* he thought to himself as he quickly paid the bill and escorted her to the elevator.

The next morning Elizabeth and Rex were cheek to cheek on the front page of *The West Australian* with the headline "Beauty and the Bowler." Elizabeth was in a complete panic as Mrs. Powell showed her the paper and told her that Mother Merrick had already called.

"I tried to assure her everything was completely proper and there was nothing to worry about, but I'm afraid she insisted you come home immediately," Mrs. Powell told her.

She knew her mother must have been furious when she saw the newspaper, and this would mean Elizabeth would never be allowed to enter another pageant again. Things had been going so well until this picture appeared. She had a wonderful evening with Rex, and he was a perfect gentlemen. They talked about his matches and his plans to travel the world. Again, she was surprised he didn't ask much about her family, which was a relief to her. She did not want him to know her family still used an outhouse and the men in her family were drunk by 6:00 p.m., and besides she loved hearing all about him. He had walked her back to the Saver Suites around 11:00 p.m. the night before and thanked Mrs. Powell for letting him spend time with her. He kissed Elizabeth on the cheek and said good night. Now Elizabeth was dreading having to leave so soon and wasn't sure she would have time to say good-bye to Rex.

The previous evening, as Rex walked back to the Royal Hotel, he felt light and happy, and a little lonely. He knew he had enjoyed Elizabeth's company but wasn't exactly sure why. She was a beautiful and pleasant girl, winner of the Miss Western Australian Pageant, and everyone who spoke with her found her completely charming. He was sure Rodney had had a great time with Sarah, and he felt a little envious, as all he had received was a thank-you when he placed a kiss on Elizabeth's cheek. "*What in the world am I so damned happy about?*" he asked himself as he went back into the bar for a nightcap.

By 9:00 a.m. that Sunday, Elizabeth was packed and saying good-bye to Mrs. Powell. She'd sent a note to the pageant committee and the mayor, telling them she had to go home ASAP due to a family matter and would not be able to attend the final cricket match. She couldn't bring herself to tell them her parents had seen the photo on the front page of *The Western Australian* and had summoned her home. She gave her sincerest apologies and also sent a note to Rex, saying she enjoyed meeting him and wished him luck in his final match. She was too embarrassed to say anything else.

Mrs. Powell had a bellboy carry the suitcases to their truck and bring it around to the front of the hotel. She wanted Elizabeth and Abby to leave as soon as possible for fear that the Merrick men would come into town to get them. She cringed at the thought of them meeting up with the cricket players and the press agents who were still in town, and she did not want any negative publicity for the Saver Suites.

Sitting in the front seat of the truck, Abby worried about what their parents would do when they arrived home. She stared at Elizabeth as she drove, trying to figure out what she was thinking. She hadn't said a word since they left Perth, and she was driving very fast. Abby just couldn't believe how quickly Mrs. Powell had their suitcases brought down to the lobby and the truck moved around in front of the hotel for them. She had been so nice to them for the last few days. Abby was very confused at what all the fuss was about. It was only a photograph, and Elizabeth had been back in their room shortly after 11:00 p.m.

Abby finally found the courage to speak to Elizabeth. "Do you think Mother will let you keep your pageant winnings?"

Elizabeth looked at her with her blue eyes wide open and a steely look of determination that would intimidate anyone and slowly said, "Well, they would have to, wouldn't they, since the check is made out to me, isn't it?" Then she smiled a strange little smile and stared at the road ahead.

In that moment Abby knew nothing was going to keep Elizabeth in Boora Rock, and Abby planned to follow as soon as she could.

They reached Boora Rock sooner than anticipated due to Elizabeth's driving speed. Their brother Karl came down the porch steps to help them with the suitcases. As Karl walked by Elizabeth he said "Nice going, Miss Western Australia."

Elizabeth ignored him and walked up the steps and said hello to everyone. Mother Merrick, her father, her brother Ed, and Father O'Malley from their church were all seated, staring at her with very somber expressions on their faces. Elizabeth said, "I'm going in to change, and I'll be down in a few moments to tell you all about it." With that, she marched into the house and climbed the stairs.

Back in Perth, the pageant committee was scrambling to find someone to sit with the mayor in his booth at the cricket game. The booth had been decorated with ribbons and a "Welcome Miss Western Australia" banner. As runner-up, and to her delight, Sarah stood in for Elizabeth with the mayor. Now that Elizabeth was out of the picture, she could focus on that handsome Rex Stewart. Her evening with Rodney had ended quickly after she let him have his way with her. She'd only done so because Rex was with Elizabeth and she thought Rodney was the second most talented player in Perth. Sarah had had enough of being second and was going to do whatever she needed to get Rex Stewart.

During breakfast in the dining room of the Royal Hotel, reporters were clambering around Rex holding copies of the paper with the photo of him and Elizabeth on the cover. They wanted to know where his beauty queen had gone and what had happened that night to make her disappear before the pageant celebrations were completed. Rex was annoyed and embarrassed by their questions because he had no idea. He received a note from her earlier that morning and was planning to talk to Mrs. Powell. Right now he had to concentrate on his game, and he was struggling with thoughts of the beautiful Elizabeth…. his beauty.

The South African Natal team won the match, and Rex set the mark for the best test performance of any bowler in South African test history. He also set the record against Australia for the most wickets taken, with thirty-two, in spite of injuring his hand midway through the series.

Later in the afternoon, as everyone celebrated in the bar, Sarah was hanging on to Rex while Rodney whispered to everyone about his evening with her. Tonight Sarah was glowing, wearing another very low-cut dress, white silk that clung to every curve on her voluptuous body and had a slit high on both sides, so when she sat on her barstool, you could see every inch of her thick white thighs.

Rex walked to the Saver Suites as soon as he could get away after the match to talk to Mrs. Powell about Elizabeth, but couldn't find her and planned to try again later that evening. The reporters would not let him forget Elizabeth, not that he could get her out of his mind. He was glad Sarah was with him that evening. He didn't want to be seen without a date, especially after his record-setting scores today. Sarah would do just fine.

A reporter made his way to the bar and asked, "So, Rex, what have you done with the beautiful Elizabeth?"

Tired of all the questions and somewhat intoxicated, he finally answered, "One doesn't kiss and tell, now does one?" He leaned into Sarah for a long, deep kiss, and she gladly reciprocated. The reporters all laughed as another photo was taken of Rex Stewart with another beautiful girl.

Rex woke up in the middle of the night to find Sarah next to him. Her dress was up around her waist, and she was lying on her side with her full, plump breasts poured onto his stomach. He had been so drunk earlier that night, all he remembered was holding Sarah's breasts as she was on top of him. He didn't remember leaving the bar or getting to his room. But right now, he wanted her off of him. Her voluptuous body was heavy, especially her legs. He slowly inched away from her and out of the bed and quickly showered and dressed. He took a last look at Sarah, her lipstick smeared and her dress gathered around her, and thought she looked better with her clothes on. He quietly pulled the door closed and made his way down the stairs to the lobby, crossed the street, and walked over to the Saver Suites to look for Mrs. Powell to find out what happened to Elizabeth.

He found her in the lobby, saying good-bye to a group of her guests. She saw him come in and smiled at him.

"I'm so glad I found you. I wanted to find out what happened to Elizabeth?" he said.

"Well, dear," she said, "I'm afraid her parents saw the picture of the two of you in the paper and called me up and told me to send her home straight away. Those Merricks are an interesting bunch over in Boora Rock, and they weren't too happy about her entering these pageants anyway. I'm afraid they are going to be even more upset when they see this morning's paper as well, Mr. Stewart."

Rex looked down at the desk and saw a picture of him kissing Sarah. This wasn't what he wanted at all. To have his picture in the paper two days in a row with beautiful women was one thing, but he was truly concerned what Elizabeth would think of him. Sarah meant nothing to him, and suddenly he was filled with concern for Elizabeth and what she would think when she saw this picture—or worse, what her family would think. From what Mrs. Powell had told him, the family was known for their flaring tempers and hard drinking. Poor Elizabeth, how would this affect her? Boora Rock was a three-hour drive east from

Perth, and Rex decided to get Rodney, borrow a car, and head out to see her before he went back to Durban. Maybe he could help her family understand things better, although he wasn't sure he understood them himself. He only knew he did not want to leave Elizabeth in an awkward situation with her family, the press, or the pageant organizers. He didn't know her address, but since the Merrick's were so well known, he thought once he made it to Boora Rock, he could ask around.

While upstairs, Elizabeth washed her face, being sure to take off all the makeup. She put on a pair of dungarees and a loosely fitting white cotton blouse and white sandals. Before she had the conversation with her family, she wanted to look like the Elizabeth they knew and not the flashy girl on the front page of *The West Australian*. She planned to stay calm and simply lay out the facts. She went back downstairs and out to the front porch, where everyone was sitting and waiting. She sat on the wicker rocker and broke the silence.

"Well, that was quite a flashy photograph, wasn't it?"

Her father was the first to respond. "Yes, it was. And could you tell us how you came to be dancing with this cricket player in a bar across the street from your hotel?"

Elizabeth took a deep breath to settle her nerves before she answered. "The pageant girls were encouraged to be friendly to everyone and to welcome them to Perth. We were the welcoming committee for the pageant and the cricket game. Mr. Stewart spoke to me at the bake sale and then invited Abby and me to brunch. We said yes, as we had worked all morning, were very hungry, and the brunch was very nice. He was a perfect gentleman. After I won the pageant, all the girls went to the lobby bar of the Royal Hotel, and Mr. Stewart volunteered to escort me. I thought it best to have an escort, and Mrs. Powell agreed, and she kept an eye on Abby. The photographer just happened to take the photo during a dance, and that's really all there is to it."

The minute the words were out of her mouth, Elizabeth saw her father's jaw tighten. She knew she appeared confidant and thought her father would appreciate her maturity and confidence, as he did with her brothers, but apparently he did not.

"Well, young lady, you have managed to put the Merrick name in the newspapers under questionable circumstances, to say the least, and exposed your little sister to a situation not befitting a young lady. Furthermore, the people in town are talking of nothing else. You are forbidden to participate in these frivolous contests in the future. I never approved of them in the first place. You may keep your prize money, and hopefully you will use better judgment in spending it than you did winning it." He rose from his chair and headed for the barn.

Elizabeth turned to her mother for support and saw none. Elizabeth got up from her chair and stormed upstairs to her room. She was hurt and angry; nothing she did was good enough for her parents. They had not even acknowledged that she actually won this contest and did not even congratulate her. They seemed so hypocritical—it was all right for her father and brothers to get drunk every night, but she was not allowed to have a nice evening out that was perfectly innocent! How could they worry about the Merrick name when it was already talked about throughout the town! She didn't know whether to cry or throw something. She was crying when sweet Abby came in and wrapped her arms around her. They sat on Elizabeth's bed with their arms around each other, feeling more trapped than ever in Boora Rock.

Rex let Rodney drive, as he had told Rex he had an aunt and uncle in Boora Rock. Rodney also told him Boora Rock was a close little community where everyone knew everyone else's business. He laughed as he said, "I'm sure the photograph of you and that beauty contest winner has the town just buzzing, as well as raising questions about her reputation."

Rex managed a weak smile, but Rodney's comments bothered him. Elizabeth was a very nice girl, and he truly felt responsible for her, and her little sister as well.

They arrived in town late in the afternoon. Rodney drove them to his aunt's house and asked where the Merricks lived. His aunt gave him the address and also offered a place for him and Rex to stay if they needed to spend the night in Boora Rock. Rex hadn't really thought about what he would say or do, but he knew he wanted to see Elizabeth again.

Abby heard the knock on the front door, and when she opened it, standing there in his tan silk suit was Rex Stewart with one of his teammates. She could see a yellow convertible parked in the road.

"Well, hello, Miss Abby. Is Elizabeth at home?" he said.

"Oh my gosh." Abby said as she let them in and turned and yelled toward the staircase, "Elizabeth, Rex Stewart is here to see you!"

Elizabeth was in her room and from her window she saw Rex and Rodney pull up in the convertible. She quickly washed her face, changed her blouse, fixed her hair, and was putting on lipstick when she heard Abby yell to her. *What would Father think now!*, Elizabeth thought to herself.

Before she reached the bottom of the stairs, she heard her father say to Rex, "So you're the bloke who has tarnished my daughter's reputation?"

Rex was visibly stunned and unprepared for this as Elizabeth entered the living room. He started to answer, when her father interrupted him and said, "Young man, I don't know you or anything about you, but I'd like to know why you've come here now. I believe you've already caused enough damage."

"Oh, Dad," Elizabeth said, "it's not like that at all..." but no one acknowledge her presence, or heard her, as Rex Stewart and Bob Merrick stared intensely at each other. It was as if neither of them was going to back down.

Rex had not come all this way to be chased off. He could imagine the publicity, as he knew back in Perth they were already wondering where he was. He stared at Bob Merrick, wondering which ship his convict relatives had come on, and said through almost gritted teeth, "I've come here to ask your permission to court your daughter." He knew now he wanted to get Elizabeth out of here. She was much too important to him to leave her behind.

Bob Merrick relaxed instantly after Rex's statement. He felt he'd shown this spoiled kid that he couldn't have any Sheila he wanted, at least not in Boora Rock. He made a motion with his hand for Rex and Rodney to have a seat, barked at Elizabeth to bring them some tinnies, and he began to display the usual Western Australian hospitality.

And bring those tinnies Elizabeth did. After an hour or so, she still had not been able to speak to Rex, and it appeared her father, Rex, and Rodney, along with her brothers, had become the best of friends. Her brother Karl had heard of Rex and knew he was a well-respected newcomer to cricket.

Another two hours passed as Elizabeth sat in the kitchen with Abby and her mother, and they listened to the men go on about cricket to football and back to cricket. Before she knew it, Rex and Rodney had had plenty to

drink and were leaving with firm handshakes all around.
Bob Merrick called for Elizabeth to say good night to Rex,
who took her on the porch and told her he would be back in
the morning to take her to the beach for a swim and a
picnic. He kissed her quickly on the cheek and then walked
unsteadily to the yellow convertible, where Rodney was
already behind the wheel.

Before he had closed the front door, her father and
brothers were saying what a great mate Rex was and how
they couldn't wait to tell their buddies at the pub about him
courting their Elizabeth. She realized at that moment all
was forgiven. Rex was a genius! He'd managed to come in
and win over her entire family—something she thought no
one would ever be able to do, especially someone from
South Africa. She was so happy as she and Abby stayed up
late into the night talking and picking out Elizabeth's outfit
for the next day.

Rex arrived the next morning in the yellow
convertible filled with an overstuffed picnic basket, towels,
and a blanket. Rodney's aunt and uncle were happy to help

out a member of South Africa's cricket team. Rodney stayed behind to visit with his family.

Rex was very happy. For the first time, he had shown concern for someone other than himself, and he felt proud that he did the right thing. He realized Elizabeth was bringing out the best in him, and he wanted to continue to feel this way. They headed to the beach and laughed as they talked about her father and brothers and all the beer they had consumed. Rex told Elizabeth that usually, whenever someone realized he was a cricket player, they would roll out the red carpet. Although, he admitted, Bob Merrick had not made it as easy for him.

Elizabeth was almost giddy; Rex had met her family and was still with her. In fact, he seemed just as happy as she was.

Rex carried everything down to the beach and laid out the blanket and towels. After they set up their picnic, they looked at the water and each other, and it was if they were reading each other's mind. They quickly took off their clothes down to their swimsuits and ran hand in hand down to the water. They dove in, and when they came up, Rex realized how truly beautiful Elizabeth was. Without her hair done up and her makeup, she was just perfect; her eyes were like shiny light-blue glass, with high cheekbones and a firm chin. Combined with her full lips and perfect white teeth, she took his breath away. Standing so close to each other in the water, still gasping for air, he put his arms around her tiny waist and kissed her. It was a deep, passionate kiss for both of them; as though they were reaching for something they wanted from each other. When their lips parted, Elizabeth looked down as if embarrassed. He took her hand and they headed back to the beach. She was so pure and innocent, he wanted to protect her and take care of her.

Rodney's aunt had packed cooked sausages, potato salad, wild tomatoes, cheese, and bread. Rex had picked up some wine on the way, which he opened, and they relaxed and drank and ate every morsel.

They spent the rest of the day talking, and Rex discovered Elizabeth was extremely well-read and very intelligent. He knew he could bring her anywhere with him and she would easily be liked and respected.

Respect…something Rex had always wanted, but had not been able to achieve. He had hoped his cricketing would bring it about, but it only helped to paint him as a playboy and an athlete. Elizabeth had presence without ever saying a word, and he admired that so much in her, especially now that he understood her humble beginnings.

When Elizabeth returned home early that evening, Abby was waiting to hear all the details of the day. Elizabeth told her she thought she was in love. "He is so handsome, charming, and a complete gentleman. What more could a girl want?" she said.

Rex had told Elizabeth he would be gone for several weeks because he was returning to South Africa early the next morning for a series of test matches against New Zealand, who would be making their first tour to South Africa. This worked well with Elizabeth's schedule, as she had several events she had to attend as part of her duties as Miss Western Australia. They agreed to meet in six weeks.

Elizabeth was looking forward to attending the events, and as usual, Abby was sent along with her.

The long tour had not dampened his competitive drive and Rex finished his outstanding performance by taking four wickets in this first-class match against New Zealand. The reporters followed him everywhere he went, all hoping to get an exclusive. Somehow they had found out that he went to Boora Rock and was officially courting Miss Elizabeth Merrick. While Rex enjoyed that publicity, and he thought of Elizabeth often, there was always a girl in the pubs who was either drunk enough or willing to discreetly tend to his physical needs. It became almost second nature to him to charm and lure the girls into his bed and even more natural for him to leave them in the morning without an ounce of remorse. He wasn't sure why he was this way with women, but he knew he would never treat his beautiful Elizabeth like that. She was too special.

CHAPTER FOUR

Rex was tired. Between the heavy schedule of the matches and the drinking and carrying on with the ladies, he was exhausted. Since he had last seen Elizabeth, he had traveled from Boora Rock to Perth back to Durban and on to England. He was trying to plan a trip to Boora Rock to see Elizabeth in between the scheduled matches, and it was very difficult. He began to question whether or not this long-distance relationship would work. But he really missed Elizabeth and wanted to see her soon.

When Rex was in Durban, he stayed with his mother, who had turned their large home into a boarding house. His mother, Kathleen Stewart, knew how to make ends meet, especially since Rex's father gambled away his earnings at the betting parlor on his way home. Joseph Stewart was a bookie, a common and accepted trade in South Africa. He had come to South Africa from England, quickly found steady employment, and was able to buy their home. Soon after the boys, Rex, Robert, and Colin, were born, his relationship with Kathleen had changed. His fun-loving Scottish wife had become materialistic and stern. Whether it was because of the position they had quickly achieved in the predominantly white British community in Durban or because of motherhood, he never knew. The only thing he was sure of was that he didn't want to go home unless the boys were home on holiday or a break from cricket. He stayed away from the house by working as much as he could and frequenting the local pubs, to make contacts, as he liked to refer to it. He avoided the pubs where his sons socialized and had a different, more colorful, group of friends he met through gambling parlors. He would only go home to bathe, sleep, and to have breakfast with Kathleen. This was their arrangement, and it suited him just fine. Joseph Stewart's life was very lonely, but he preferred it to all of Kathleen's machinations.

Rex loved Durban. Growing up in this beautiful part of South Africa on the shores of the Indian Ocean, and only a few hours from the Drakensberg mountain ranges near the game reserves, and occasionally going on safari, was every young boy's dream. He and his brothers fished, hunted, fought, and, of course, played cricket. Their parents did not encourage them in their education, but did encourage their cricket. Rex always thought it was strange to be made fun of when he was reading, as did Robert when he tried to learn to play the clarinet. Their parents enjoyed seeing their sons' names in the papers reporting on their cricket scores, and being interviewed by reporters quite frequently. The notoriety of the Stewart name was very gratifying to them, especially Kathleen.

It would be three months before Rex made it back to Boora Rock. Without the money to travel on his own, he had to wait until the South African cricket club had a match against Australia. They were playing in Melbourne, and after much pleading, he managed to convince Rodney to take him to Perth. It was convenient, as they stayed with Rodney's family in Boora Rock again, so expenses were minimal for Rex. Rodney's family was quite wealthy from sugar cane farming, and he received an allowance, which was something Rex envied. Thanks to the generosity of his friend, it was also a source of cash for Rex. Cricket players were not paid a wage, but the clubs paid all of their expenses. Successful players usually made their fortunes by endorsing products, becoming spokesmen for large corporations, or once they retired, becoming sports announcers. Rex had not been approached for any of this work yet, which was why he was working so hard to beat bowling scores.

Elizabeth had been busy with photo shoots for the Pageant sponsors, product advertising, and was a guest on a few radio programs. Because of her charming and graceful personality, she was liked by everyone, and her name was becoming well-known throughout Western Australia. She had received a few notes and phone calls from Rex over the last few months, the last of which had made her very happy. He was coming to Western Australia for a test match and would be able to see her for two days. She could hardly wait to see her handsome South African! Although, since becoming Miss Western Australia, she had accepted invitations to go on quite a few other dates. After all, she and Rex were not exclusive and deep down she harbored a doubt if Rex truly would come back to her. There was a young doctor in Perth she had met at a medical convention she was asked to host who had become quite taken with her. But Elizabeth could not get Rex off her mind.

Rex arrived in Boora Rock and was surprised to find the press there waiting for him. Apparently they had heard through the Merrick clan he was coming to see Elizabeth, and they loved the tale of the beauty queen and the cricket player. Rex was surprised to discover that, since he had been gone, Elizabeth had become almost as famous as he was. He also heard that she had been seen on a few dates with someone else, and this greatly disturbed him. For two days, Elizabeth and Rex spent every moment they could together. Although between the Merrick's and the press, it became a game for them to see how they could elude everyone and steal a few tender moments and kisses in private.

At Rodney's aunt's house late in the evenings, Rex missed Elizabeth. He didn't want to be away from her for very long, and when she was near him, he thought of no one else, which he knew was unusual for him. He did not like it that she would date someone else when he was away. He dreaded going back to South Africa without her, and the traveling back and forth was challenging. Suddenly, it came to him, and he came up with a plan to make things easier for everyone, especially him and Elizabeth. He had made up his mind, and that was it. He was going to ask Elizabeth to marry him. He loved her. He was sure of it, as she had added something to his life no woman had ever done before—respect. He wanted it, he needed it, and Elizabeth, with all her intelligence, charm, and grace, would help him get it. He was thrilled and quite pleased with his decision.

He arranged for a quiet dinner for the two of them at the Boora Rock Inn. Fortunately, the owner was a cricket fan, and when Rex told him his plans to propose to Boora Rock's own Elizabeth Merrick, he suggested a small private dining room. The innkeeper was excited and happy to help, and he offered to handle everything for Rex. Rex, of course, graciously agreed.

That afternoon Rex met with Bob Merrick to ask for his daughter's hand in marriage. Bob was delighted, especially when Rex suggested she come back to Durban, South Africa, with him and stay at his mother's boarding house until the wedding could be arranged. Rex knew his mother would throw a grand wedding reception, and he wanted to get married in South Africa. He also secretly hoped the press would cover the event. Bob was happy and relieved, as this took a great weight off his shoulders because he could not afford a wedding for either of his daughters. With Elizabeth going to Durban for the wedding, it saved him the cost and the embarrassment in Boora Rock. Both men agreed, and with a handshake, Elizabeth's fate was sealed.

The glow from over one hundred white candles lit the room that was filled with dozens of white and red roses. When Rex escorted Elizabeth into the private room with mahogany walls and crown molding, and a small fireplace in the middle of the largest wall, it literally took her breath away. The room had a delicate scent from the flowers and

67

seemed to glow from the all candlelight. In the center was a small table draped with a white cloth completely set for dinner—for two. She also noticed the bottle of champagne chilling in a bucket near the table.

Elizabeth was glad she had worn the red cocktail dress from the fashion show she had on when she first met Rex. When he called her earlier that day, he told her he was taking her to dinner and to dress up. When she saw this beautiful room, she was happy with her choice.

She sensed Rex was nervous. He pulled out her chair for her and poured them both a glass of the chilled champagne.

"I hope you are pleased," he said. "I wanted a special evening for us."

"It's the most beautiful setting I have ever seen," she said.

"Elizabeth, I had a talk with your father today, and—"

"Oh God!" she interrupted, "I can only imagine what he said. Honestly, I never know what he might say." Suddenly she was worried her father had said something to scare Rex away, maybe divulging too much about the family's past, as they could actually be traced back to one of the original convict ships from England, or worse, maybe he had let Rex know of his depleted financial situation. She prayed he had not asked Rex for a loan.

"Actually, we had a very pleasant conversation. You see, Elizabeth, I think you and I should get married," he said bluntly.

Elizabeth was stunned. Not so much by what Rex had said, but by the way he said it. She waited to see if he would say something else, like how much he loved and wanted her, but nothing else was said. He was just looking at her, waiting for a response. She needed more from him, so she slowly asked, "Why do you think that?"

He leaned forward in his chair and eagerly replied, "We are good for one another, Elizabeth, and I believe together we can both get what we want and get along quite nicely. I adore you and can't imagine being married to anyone else, and the press just loves us together. I know you would like to leave Boora Rock and travel, and with me, you can. I would like you to come back to South Africa with me and stay at my mother's boarding house until we can be married, as I will not be back in Australia for quite some time, and I can't imagine going back without you. Your father has already given his approval. So, what do you say, Elizabeth? Will you marry me?"

It was not the proposal or expression of love she had always hoped for and dreamed of, but she knew in his own way he loved her. In fact, she was flattered he trusted her so much and thought of her as a friend as well as a woman. He was staring at her with his beautiful blue eyes and an awkward, nervous smile on his face. She almost saw the child in him, and she loved him so deeply. "Yes, Rex Stewart, I will marry you."

Then he stood up and took her into his arms and gave her the most passionate kiss he had even given her, or anyone. Their tall, slender bodies were pressed closely together with their arms wrapped tightly around each other. They both felt the passion burning in them, and at that moment, they wanted only each other for the rest of their lives. Rex pulled back and told her he had made his decision to ask her on this trip and had not had time to get her a ring, as there weren't any places in Boora Rock that offered what he wanted. He promised her when they got to Durban he would present her with a sparkling engagement ring. They dined and sipped the champagne and talked into the late hours of the night about their plans, their future, and their arrangement. They were both completely happy with each other and the choice they had made.

When he brought her back to her parents' home, it was almost 2:00 a.m., and they were surprised to find them waiting in the living room. Rex said, "Elizabeth has agreed to marry me."

There were hugs and kisses all around, and as Elizabeth hugged her father, she said quietly to him, "I'm so happy, Dad."

No one noticed Abby sitting at the top of the stairs.

The next morning, unbeknownst to Elizabeth, Rex and her father had made all of the arrangements for their trip to South Africa. They would leave the next day on a flight from Perth to Madagascar and then another flight to Durban. To Rex's relief, Bob Merrick managed to hand him a small amount of money to help with travel expenses. He was hoping the club would pick up the rest of the expenses as they welcomed his fiancé.

Elizabeth felt like a princess. Her prince had come to save her. He was whisking her away and taking care of everything. She packed all that she owned, which sadly filled up only a small makeup case and her large, old red suitcase. She told Rex she would send for the rest of her things to save herself any embarrassment. They set the wedding date for the first of June in Durban. Elizabeth would stay with Rex's mother until he finished his tour, and this would allow Elizabeth time to get to know his family and the city of Durban and plan the wedding.

Abby was upstairs in the room she had shared with Elizabeth all her life. She was truly happy her sister was leaving Boora Rock, getting married and moving to an exciting place like Durban, South Africa. She also realized she would be alone with her parents and brothers for the first time. She started crying, but wasn't sure if it was out of joy for her sister or sadness for herself.

Elizabeth came into the room and looked at her little sister crying and knew what she was thinking. She sat on the bed and hugged her tight and whispered to her, "I will send for you as soon as you graduate from high school, I promise you."

The following morning, Rodney, Rex, and Elizabeth drove to the Perth Airport in the yellow convertible. Upon their arrival, the press swarmed their car and followed them as they unloaded their bags and entered the airport. They had apparently seen *The West Australian* headline that read "Miss Western Australia and South African Cricket Player to Wed." The young couple didn't answer any questions, but smiled as they posed for a few photographs. It was a long flight from Perth to Madagascar, but Elizabeth was so excited about starting her new life, she was not at all concerned.

Rex's brothers, Robert and Colin, met them in Durban to drive them to the family home. Elizabeth instantly liked Robert. He was tall, handsome, and quite sophisticated. He chatted with Rex and politely made small talk with Elizabeth. He made her feel very welcomed and was kind and gentle compared to her own brothers' crass behavior. Colin, on the other hand, made Elizabeth uncomfortable. He was the youngest and surprisingly short, but handsome nonetheless. He was also a cricket player and knew he was liked by the ladies and made a lot of off-color jokes that Elizabeth didn't find particularly funny. Colin had loaded their bags into the trunk of his red convertible and moved the seat so Elizabeth could get into the backseat with Robert. Elizabeth sat quietly in the back, wondering if all cricket players drove convertibles, and she wondered what color convertible Rex drove.

Kathleen Stewart was a tall, slim, red-haired woman with blue eyes and a thick Scottish accent. She hugged and kissed Rex like a son who had just come home from war. She said a quick but polite hello to Elizabeth and asked Colin to have a servant bring in the bags. Elizabeth quickly discovered Rex had not told his mother of their plans when he introduced her simply as Miss Elizabeth Merrick. They were taken into a large square room with shiny hardwood floors and red Persian rugs. In the center of the room facing each other were two long red-and-gold floral print sofas. The room had a large brick fireplace and next to it were two gold Queen Anne chairs. There were many antiques in the room, including an antique roll-top desk tucked away in one corner of the room, and a long, cushioned wooden bench against the longest wall. There was a door that led to a screened veranda with dark wicker furniture with glass-covered table tops. The veranda seemed to wrap around the entire house. Combined, these rooms provided ample seating. A barefoot black woman served tea. She was dressed in a simple white cotton blouse and skirt and had a white cap on her head to hold her hair in place. She silently set the tea tray on the table.

Rex gulped his tea and set his cup down and said to his mother, "Elizabeth and I are engaged, Mother, and I've brought her here to stay with you while I play in the next test match."

Kathleen's blue eyes grew large as her eyebrows rose in surprise. She stumbled to find the appropriate words as she said, "Oh, well, um, congratulations, son, and to you, Elizabeth. This is quite a surprise."

Missing were the hugs and kisses they had received at the Merrick home, and Elizabeth knew Kathleen was not pleased. She also noticed Rex seemed indifferent to his mother's reaction as he poured himself another cup of tea and reached for a piece of shortbread. He proceeded to tell her how they met and how they wanted to be married on June 1, in her home. By now, Elizabeth was feeling embarrassed that Rex was springing all of his plans on his mother, but respected the graceful way she responded to her son.

"I would love to help you and your fiancée, and, of course, you must have the wedding here. We will have a grand celebration." She smiled at everyone and quietly finished her tea.

As Elizabeth expected, the house was large and beautiful. It was no wonder Rex's mother had turned it into a boarding house. She converted some of the larger rooms into smaller single bedrooms, and it was in one of these where she placed Elizabeth's luggage. It was also at the opposite end of the house and the furthest away from Rex's bedroom. To Elizabeth's surprise, the servants had unpacked her bags, and her sparse belongings were neatly hung in the closet or folded in the dresser drawers. Even her makeup had been unpacked and neatly arranged on the small vanity. Elizabeth thought she was going to love it here, but was not so sure how she would get along with Kathleen.

After she instructed her two house servants to clear the tea and went over the dinner menu with them, Kathleen went to her room and lay down on her bed. Her worst fear was about to come true—her precious Rex, her shining star, was about to marry someone beneath him. Yes, the girl was pretty and poised, but poor. All of Kathleen's hopes for Rex to marry someone with a better social standing and accompanying wealth were about to be ruined. She had three months to see that it did not happen.

That evening they dined in the dining room that was large enough to seat fourteen people comfortably. They were also joined by two of the boarders, Miss Anna Hunter, a writer from London who loved to go to the beach to work on her book. She had a cousin who lived nearby with eight children, with little room for her to stay with them. Mrs. Stewart gladly took her in. The second boarder was Mr. Albert Stonely, who had recently been transferred from Johannesburg and worked at the local radio station, in the sports department. Both of Kathleen's boarders loved to hear about the Stewart sons' cricketing and, to Kathleen's delight, were happy to promote them within their circle of friends and business acquaintances.

They were served roast beef with gravy, fresh green beans, scalloped potatoes, a salad from Kathleen's garden, and for dessert, chocolate cake. The latter a favorite, Elizabeth learned, of her future husband's.

It was a talkative and lively dinner group. Kathleen noticed how easily Elizabeth talked with everyone on the different topics discussed and could see why Rex was attracted to her. Elizabeth and Kathleen barely spoke directly to each other, but it was a pleasant evening for all.

After dinner, Rex took Elizabeth for a walk around the property, which was directly across the road separating them from a sandy white beach and ocean. Then they sat on a love seat on the terrace that overlooked the perfectly manicured lawns. They embraced and kissed, but were constantly interrupted by Colin, Miss Hunter, Mr. Stonely, Kathleen, and the servants. It was a busy house when everyone was home. Rex promised to take Elizabeth into town the next day and to show her some of his favorite places.

Elizabeth excused herself around 10:00 p.m. and went up to her room. She didn't realize how tired she was from the long trip until she woke up late the next afternoon. By the time she went downstairs, Kathleen was sitting in the living room having afternoon tea. She motioned for Elizabeth to take a seat on the sofa opposite her and asked one of the servants to bring Elizabeth a sandwich with her tea.

"You must be exhausted from your trip."

"Yes, it was a rather long flight."

"I have never been to Australia or traveled much, except when we came to Durban. My sons travel quite a bit with their cricketing. The house is so quiet now," she said.

Elizabeth thanked her for the tea and sandwich, but didn't respond to her comments, as she seemed sad that her sons were no longer at home with her.

While Elizabeth ate her food, Kathleen asked, "Is your family planning to come to the wedding?"

Elizabeth realized, with all the well-wishes and the whirlwind travel arrangements, they hadn't really had time to discuss it. "You know," she said, "I don't know. With all the confusion and rush before we left, we didn't get a chance to talk about it. I will write to them straightaway." Although, thinking of it now, Elizabeth knew her family would not be with her on her wedding day, as they could not afford the cost of the long trip.

"Do you have many brothers and sisters?" Kathleen asked, thinking the Australians were known for their fun-loving nature and forthright ways.

"Yes," Elizabeth said, "I have four brothers and a younger sister." She felt uncomfortable with Kathleen and was being careful to use proper manners and grammar when she spoke. She was annoyed with herself that she was letting this woman make her nervous, and she didn't care if she was Rex's mother. She had barely finished the sandwich when another question came. She felt they were questions, and not friendly conversation, and that bothered her.

"How did you come to be a contestant in the Miss Western Australia pageant, Elizabeth?" Kathleen asked. She was wondering if Elizabeth had been nominated or, worse, applied for it and was using her beauty to advance herself.

Elizabeth inhaled and said, "Well, I was working as a cashier in the McGhee's Department Store on Saturdays for extra spending money, and they asked me to model some of the dresses for the ladies. Then they wanted to use my photograph in their advertisements for those dresses, and some of the other local merchants approached me as well. One of the store owners was on the pageant committee, and she encouraged me to submit an application. I did so just to please her, and I was really surprised when I was accepted. Things just sort of blossomed from there, really."

Just then Rex came downstairs carrying his suitcase. Elizabeth also noticed another one by the door and assumed Colin was leaving as well. "Well, I'm off to the test match in Johannesburg, and I will be back in three weeks." He bent down to kiss his mother on the cheek and then took Elizabeth's hands as she stood up. He whispered to her "Three weeks my beauty", he kissed her and held her for a long moment. They were interrupted as Rodney was knocking on the door. The three cricketers loaded up the car and were gone.

Elizabeth realized Rex had forgotten his promise to show her around Durban. And she also realized she would be alone with Kathleen.

Fortunately, Elizabeth adapted well to her new surroundings. She was glad Miss Hunter and Mr. Stonely were there for meals and in the evenings. Elizabeth and Miss Hunter became friends, even venturing into Durban to do some shopping using some of her pageant winnings.

Elizabeth was anxious to discuss wedding plans with Kathleen, but she seemed in no hurry to plan anything, often saying, "June is still a long way away, dear. We have plenty of time."

During the weeks Rex was away, Elizabeth and Miss Hunter also went to the Indian Market, where Elizabeth discovered the Indians, in particular, the Indian women. She was appalled at their constant black tongues, which she assumed came from the nuts they were always chewing. They sold their goods at an open-air market in downtown Durban. You could buy all sorts of items, such as shoes, bags, fabric, pots, and spices. The curry powder, with its pungent odor, was particularly noticeable, but she discovered she loved its flavor. Elizabeth bought linens and pots and stored them in her room at the Stewart house.

Kathleen realized Rex would be home in a few days from his latest trip, and for weeks now he seemed to be ignoring her letters urging him to cancel the wedding and take Elizabeth back to Australia. Although she had made little effort to spend any real time getting to know Elizabeth, she decided to have tea with her again in the hopes of handling some small wedding detail so she would have something to report to Rex.

Elizabeth felt she was being summoned like a child and was growing to despise "tea." She told Kathleen she wanted to keep the wedding small and simple. She had written to her family, and as she suspected, they would not be able to attend the wedding. She was so sad Abby would not be her maid of honor as they had always planned. Kathleen agreed to the simple wedding, and the two of them decided on hors d'oeuvres, champagne, and cake. Kathleen was shocked when Elizabeth informed her she would make her own wedding dress from a beautiful fabric she had bought at the Indian Market.

When Elizabeth first arrived in Durban almost three months ago, she had $3,000, the entire amount she had won as Miss Western Australia. She used a small amount at the Indian Market and planned to use a small portion for the wedding expenses, which would leave her a nice amount to put away for a rainy day. However, she was quite taken aback when Kathleen handed her a guest list of nearly a hundred people. It included the entire Stewart family in South Africa, cricket club members and players, local politicians, and members of the press. Kathleen was turning her wedding into a promotional event, and Elizabeth was spitting mad. She looked forward to becoming Mrs. Rex Stewart and leaving Kathleen's house as soon as possible.

Rex had been home several times in the last three months, but not for long, usually only for a few days at a time. Elizabeth had tried to talk to him about his mother's apparent dislike for her, but he would only say, "Don't worry. We will be married soon enough, and she will just have to accept it. Besides, I am sure in time she will grow to love you as I do."

Elizabeth wanted to believe him, but looked forward to the day they would be on their own.

Rex was returning home very pleased with his game. He was becoming well-known and sought after and had played for several teams, including Natal, Rhodesia, and Transvaal. However, he was tired from the traveling, drinking and the frolicking with women he encountered along the way. He laughed as he thought how ironic it was he should have run into the busty Sarah again, and she was just as scrumptious but disappointing as she had been the first time. More than ever he was looking forward to marrying Elizabeth and settling down a bit. He felt no guilt about the women he was with when he was traveling because they meant nothing to him. After all, Elizabeth was not his wife yet, and when she was, he would change his behavior. Besides, Elizabeth was a virgin and never let things get too heated when they were alone. He was sure once they were married, everything would change for both of them.

CHAPTER FIVE

The cooler air had arrived, and it was exactly one week until the wedding. Rex was planning to be home within the next few days and was eager to finalize his plans for their honeymoon. The South African cricket club had heard of Rex's impending marriage and had reserved the honeymoon cabin at The Cavern for them with all meals and drinks included. It was a beautiful and quiet location, high in the mountains of Drakensberg. It was very secluded, with a wonderful restaurant, lounge, pools, and tennis courts, exactly the kind of environment Rex wanted for his honeymoon with Elizabeth.

On the morning of June 1, the weather was just beautiful. Although it was almost winter in South Africa, the temperature had risen to seventy-two degrees Fahrenheit, and there was a warm, soft breeze. Kathleen had a large white open-air tent erected on the lawn, under which the ceremony would take place. The buffet and bar were located in the back of the tent, and on the right side, a small band was setting up their instruments. A dance floor was placed in the center of the tent, and tables with white linens, flowers, and covered chairs were arranged around the two open sides of the dance floor. All of this was a wedding present from Kathleen.

Elizabeth had worked for weeks on her dress, which was made of silk with a touch of lace. It was a low-cut off-the-shoulder gown, fitted tightly at her waist, which flowed to the floor with a small train. For her hair, she chose a small band of miniature white roses. Simple but tasteful, even Kathleen agreed. Colin was the best man, and Elizabeth had asked Miss Hunter to stand up for her. Elizabeth and Rex had met with the minister the day before and selected a short ceremony, neither of them wanting to show too much of their emotion in public. Elizabeth asked Robert to give her away. She liked him, and he had always treated her with respect and kindness. He was deeply touched she had asked him, and he gladly accepted.

As she walked down the short aisle to meet Rex, she was transfixed by his deep blue eyes. He was smiling at her, and she instinctively smiled back. As Robert let go of her arm, Rex reached for her hand. They gazed into each other's eyes throughout the entire ceremony, both of them relieved when it was over. Rex pulled her close and gave her a long, deep kiss. When they parted, flashbulbs blinded them as cameras captured the happy couple walking down the aisle as husband and wife. It all happened so quickly, or so it seemed…Colin making a toast, the band playing a waltz, and many more photographs. Elizabeth thought it was almost déjà vu of last summer, when they had danced at the pageant reception and the flashbulbs went off.

Kathleen was very pleased with the guest attendance, the reception, and of course, the publicity for her son. She even gave Elizabeth warm congratulations as they departed. Maybe Elizabeth could help her son after all, she thought.

Colin was driving them directly to Drakensberg, his date in the front seat with him. Rex and Elizabeth were tucked in the back with a bottle of champagne. Elizabeth felt light-headed as Rex kissed her and his hands roamed over her gown and her body for the first time. Elizabeth felt her body tingle as Rex kissed her and touched her, and she couldn't believe how happy she was as Mrs. Rex Stewart. Colin delivered them at The Cavern and made sure their cabin was ready before he headed back to Durban. As they signed in, their bags were taken to their cabin along with a cold bottle of champagne and a welcome basket of fruits, cheeses, and breads. Rex carried his beautiful new bride over the threshold and closed the door. He poured them each another glass of the champagne and made a toast "to the most perfect woman in the world for me."

Although she was already light-headed, Elizabeth clinked his glass and drank her champagne. She was very nervous as he put his glass on a nearby table and then put his arms around her waist and kissed her again.

He had waited so long for this moment. He wanted to ravish her, but was mindful of her innocence, so he chose to take each step slowly and deliberately. His kisses were softer as his lips moved to her neck. He slowly turned her around and carefully unzipped her gown, and it fell slightly off her shoulder. His lips slowly moved to the exposed skin.

She turned to him, and this time she kissed him with a passion she had never felt before.

Sensing her eagerness, he guided her dress off her shoulders and down her arms until it fell to the floor. He bent down and gently lifted each foot to allow her to step out of her dress, leaving her high heels on. To his delight, Elizabeth turned and began to unbutton his shirt, and she pushed it back to expose his strong chest. He gazed at her and thought she was truly the most magnificent woman he had ever seen. Standing before him in her bra, panties, stockings, and heels, she was exquisite. Her breasts were pushed up and were soft to his lips as he pulled her to him and kissed them.

She was trembling and felt her legs go weak as Rex lifted her onto the bed and unhooked her bra and removed it. She reached to unhook his belt as he removed her white lace panties.

Elizabeth wanted him as he climbed on her and kissed her lips and neck. She was aching to feel him on her, and she gasped as the young couple became one.

He was very gentle with his new bride and slowly began to move with a rocking motion that made her want him even more.

He felt her release as he pressed his full weight against her and she grabbed his back and pulled him down further to her. She wanted him. His beauty was responding to him as he knew she would. They moved together as one, and both were panting heavily, until they gasped in unison and released the passion that they had felt for each other for so long. Elizabeth felt his warmth within her, and tears of joy filled her eyes as she held on to him tightly.

The newlyweds lay still as they caught their breath. Elizabeth looked at her handsome new husband, and then at herself, and burst out laughing as she realized she had nothing on but stockings and shoes. Rex laughed, too, as he rolled over and took his bride again.

The happy couple was the talk of The Cavern as they played tennis, went hiking, and were seen cavorting in the pool late one night. Elizabeth felt a freedom with Rex she had never known before and was happier than she had imagined possible. Her husband seemed pleased with her and was kind and gentle and allowed her to explore him at her own pace. Her natural curiosity led her to places on her husband's body she had only read about. She wanted to give herself to him and was glad she enjoyed every part of him and wanted to spend every moment with him. She loved him and trusted him completely.

Rex was happy, too, that his new bride was everything he had hoped for. She was curious and adventuresome in their bed, and he was delighted. He really loved his beautiful wife. They ate, slept, and made love several times a day, some days never leaving their cabin.

As they sat on the lawn overlooking the mountains the day before they were to leave, Elizabeth asked, "Where are we going to live when we get back to Durban?"

"Well, I thought we would stay with my mother until we can afford a place of our own."

Elizabeth's heart sank as she said, "Oh, no, Rex, I can't. I don't think I could stay at your mother's again. I really can't."

"We don't have a choice, Elizabeth; I have to find a way to save some money to get us a place of our own."

"Couldn't we at least take a small apartment in town until we can buy something? I have some money left from the pageant. What do you have saved?"

For the first time, Rex seemed irritated as he huffed, "I have nothing saved. I have nothing. My brothers know a few chaps, and I will enlist their help in finding a place for us. I'm sure it's only a matter of time before I secure a product endorsement, as my scores have been very good lately."

As disappointed and surprised as Elizabeth was, she was determined not to go back to Kathleen's. "When we get back to Durban, I am going to find a small apartment, and if I have to, I will get a job until you can work something out."

"I'll take care of everything, Elizabeth. Don't worry. We will not be in this situation for long."

"Well, we are in this together, aren't we?"

"Yes, my beauty, we are."

That evening, as Elizabeth soaked in a hot bath, she evaluated her situation and her marriage. She assumed whatever money he did have he was using for their honeymoon. She was glad she hadn't asked too many questions during their conversation, as he was clearly embarrassed. She loved Rex, there was no doubt. She only wished he had discussed his financial situation with her sooner, as she might have waited to come to South Africa until he had saved for their marriage. Now she found herself in a strange country, living with a mother-in-law she didn't like, desperate to find another place to live, and faced with finding employment. She was disappointed, but not daunted. She had married well and had seen enough of the press surround Rex to know it was just a matter of time before a contract was offered to him.

Rex went down to The Cavern's lounge and was having a drink and talking to some of the other guests while he waited for Elizabeth. He knew she was disappointed, but thought she handled the truth quite well. In fact, he was glad she knew. He wondered if she would have been so quick to agree to marry him had she known beforehand. Just then Elizabeth walked into the lounge, and Rex noticed every man in the room look at his wife. They enjoyed their last evening in Drakensberg and ended their honeymoon as they had begun, with a glass of champagne and a night of passionate lovemaking.

CHAPTER SIX

To Elizabeth's dismay, they walked back into Kathleen's house exactly eight days after their wedding. Kathleen was thrilled to see her son and was her usual cordial self toward Elizabeth. After dinner that night, Elizabeth asked Miss Hunter if her cousin might know of any apartments for lease downtown. Kathleen was clearly annoyed when Elizabeth also asked Mr. Stonely if he knew of any available apartment in the area.

The next day Rex headed to Cape Town to play against England. Colin and Robert joined him for the trip, as Robert was playing, and they would be back in six days. Elizabeth sent her husband off with a big hug, and kisses, and went straight to the living room to get the newspaper and started to search the classified ads for apartments. She found two she wanted to see, and Miss Hunter agreed to go with her.

The first one was very small and close to the Indian street market, and as much as Elizabeth enjoyed shopping there, she didn't want to live above it. The second was a one-bedroom on the second floor of an old building. It was a corner unit, and it had big windows on all sides. The kitchen was small, but it had a large living room and bedroom. The manager was asking $250 per month and wanted two months in advance. It was a great location close to the beach and downtown. The building itself was a sturdy four-story built in the 1920s. With a little paint, curtains, and furniture it would be perfect. She loved it and knew Rex would too. She noticed a young couple downstairs waiting to see the apartment next. The manager could not hold it until Rex came back, so Elizabeth agreed to take it on the spot. She had her money with her and gave him $750 knowing she still had enough left to help furnish it and thinking Rex could take over from there until she found a job. The manager asked her to sign a lease he had drafted, and once he filled in her name, she happily signed it. She and Rex could finally leave Kathleen's and really start their lives together.

For the next two days, Elizabeth cleaned and painted the apartment while she waited for Rex to return. He called her once, and she told him about their new apartment. He was silent at first, and she thought he was upset that she had signed the lease.

South Africa lost the match to England that day. Hanging up the phone Rex realized Elizabeth had not even asked him about it. His temporary silence on the phone earlier wasn't about a lease, but the reality of being responsible for a wife and finding a way to pay for an apartment. But she was so excited, and hearing her on the phone, he told her he couldn't wait to see it.

He drank so much that night he was carried to his room by his brothers. They were wondering just what Rex had gotten himself into. So was his sponsor, John Macheeth.

Fearful his rising star would become too distracted to concentrate on his bowling, he told Rex the next morning when they got back to Durban he should take his beautiful wife to the local furniture store and select whatever they needed to rent for their apartment, courtesy of the club for the next six months. Rex was visibly relieved, and that afternoon he again set the best mark for bowlers, taking 48 wickets at 18.75, the best he ever had.

By the time Rex came home from Cape Town, Elizabeth had finished cleaning and paining the apartment. She had enlisted the help of Mr. Stonely one afternoon, and he helped her to bring the pots, pans, linens, and other few household items she purchased from the Indian Market over the last few months. Kathleen was cold to Elizabeth and did not offer any assistance to help the newlyweds get set up in their new home. Elizabeth asked Kathleen one day if she would like to see the apartment, but she quickly declined, stating she was just too busy.

Rex took Elizabeth to the furniture store John Macheeth had recommended. The store owner was more than happy to help one of South Africa's finest. Elizabeth selected a pink-and-maroon flowered sofa, a large maroon-and-green striped chair, and glass coffee and end tables. She also picked a small dining room set, a bedroom set with nightstands, lamps, and a radio and record console. She was thrilled—her first home!

Rex took the owner aside to discuss the cost of the items, and the owner said, "It has all been taken care of. You have no payments for six months. However, after that, just come in and make a minimal payment each month. I'm happy to help you, son."

Rex shook his hand, and that afternoon everything was delivered to their apartment. That evening Elizabeth cooked them their first dinner and burned the lamp chops. She cried and became frustrated, but Rex took her into his arms and told her he wasn't hungry anyway. He couldn't help but smile and be amused by his sweet wife. They grabbed two spoons and shared a carton of chocolate ice cream for dinner. Later they made love in their home, feeling closer than they ever had. Elizabeth cuddled next to her husband, happy to have him all to herself.

CHAPTER SEVEN

Six weeks later, Rex was happy to be on his way back to England. He was feeling isolated and cooped up all this time in the apartment with Elizabeth. He loved his wife, but was tired of talking about curtains and fretting over burned dinners. Rodney was in the seat next to him as they enjoyed several scotches on the rocks on their long flight.

Elizabeth had been looking for work in Durban to help with expenses, as Rex never seemed to have cash to help with groceries and household expenses. She hated to trouble him because she knew he was paying for the furniture and trying to concentrate on his bowling. When he was home, he listened intently to the radio when there was a game being broadcast and kept track of his competitors' performances. She finally found a job at an upscale dress shop on Grey Street, near their apartment. It worked out better than she expected, as the owner asked Elizabeth to wear their dresses at work, loaning her five dresses, and asked her to eventually buy one or two herself. They felt Elizabeth was just the image they wanted for their customers and knew her stunning good looks in their dresses would help their sales.

One morning, a few weeks after she started work at the shop, Elizabeth became very nauseous and felt faint. She didn't think much of it, other than she did not eat much when Rex was away.

After watching Elizabeth like this for two days, the shop owner, Mrs. Martin, a kind and elegant woman from Manchester, asked, "Do you think you might be pregnant, dear?"

It hadn't even occurred to Elizabeth, as she assumed she had caught the flu. She thought about it as she sat down in a nearby chair, feeling queasy. "I suppose it is possible. I probably should go and see a doctor."

Mrs. Martin recommended a doctor, and Elizabeth went the next day and discovered she was six weeks pregnant. She cried when the doctor told her, but wasn't sure why, and she felt very embarrassed. She was completely surprised and couldn't wait to tell Rex. She thought she was a little late in her cycle, but attributed it to the stress of setting up house and trying to find work. She decided she would tell him in person when he came home. Mrs. Martin believed Elizabeth would not begin to show for another three months because she was so slim and this was her first baby. She assured Elizabeth she would keep her on until the baby came.

That evening, thinking of her baby, Elizabeth made herself a steak and boiled a potato. She ate alone, which was common when Rex was away. She thought of calling Kathleen to tell her she was pregnant, but decided against it. She would wait for Rex; he would make her feel better about everything.

During his second tour of the United Kingdom, Rex bowled excellently again in a series of first-class matches. He took 153 wickets at 14.72, marking the best performance by a South African bowler since 1912. He was really enjoying himself and it felt good to be playing. He was bowling well, and it was great to be with the boys.

He felt relaxed with them, and they understood him like no one else. They played hard during the day and drank and joked all night. They also enjoyed the flirtatious women who always gathered around the players. One, in particular, was a beautiful blonde name Joan. She was about twenty, pleasant, and playful, and Rex couldn't stop staring at her. She was obviously soaking up the attention the guys showered on her. She had been talking to Rex, but after John Macheeth told her he was a newlywed, she paid little attention to him. Rex stumbled to his room that night, drunk and alone.

Back in Durban, Elizabeth prepared a dinner of curry chicken after a long day at the dress shop. For the past few days, she'd been craving curry even though the odor made her nauseous. Rex was due home that evening, and she was going to tell him about the baby.

When he came home and walked through the kitchen door, he thought Elizabeth looked pale. Elizabeth ran to Rex, threw her arms around her husband, and kissed his neck and face. Tears welled in her eyes as he gave her a long and passionate kiss. He was glad to see his beautiful wife.

"How are you, my beauty? I've missed you."

"I'm fine. I've been busy with my work at the dress shop and finishing things here in the apartment."

"Yes." He looked around. "Everything looks really wonderful. It is good to be home. You look pale, my

beauty. Are you feeling okay?"

"Well, um, not really, I have been to see the doctor."

"What is it, my dear? What's wrong?"

"The doctor says I'm going to have a baby. You are going to be a father in about eight months."

Although surprised, Rex smiled and lifted Elizabeth off her feet and spun her around.

"A baby, isn't that something? A little one running around. Have you told Mother?"

"No, I wanted to tell you first."

"We must ring her up. She will be absolutely thrilled. Her first grandchild!"

107

Rex thought a grandchild would please his mother and stop her letters and phone calls encouraging him to annul his marriage. He never told Elizabeth about his mother's interfering, and he hoped when the baby was born, this would finally bring his mother and Elizabeth closer.

For the next few months Rex was home, he secretly worried about how he would provide for Elizabeth and the baby. He got a part-time job at the Durban High School, helping coach the cricket team. He liked working with the young men who would be the next generation of cricketers. He noticed some of them could bat and bowl as well as some of the club players and very soon would be recruited themselves. After work, he would stop at his favorite pub and have a few cocktails with the other club players who were also home, and of course, his brother Colin was always ready for a drink and a cricket story.

Elizabeth's pregnancy was an easy one. Having Rex at home calmed her, and she blossomed nicely as she prepared for the arrival of their baby. However, she knew having Rex home with her would be short-lived, as he was headed back to England very soon.

CHAPTER EIGHT

It was very early one morning some months later, as Elizabeth lay in her bed, writhing with pain. Rex left for England a few weeks before, and Elizabeth was panicking. The baby was early; she was only in her eighth month. She got up from the bed to phone Robert, who was not on the tour this time, and she felt her water break, forming a puddle at her feet. Robert was at Kathleen's house and said he would be there as quick as he could. To Elizabeth's dismay, he arrived within twenty minutes with Kathleen in tow. The last thing she wanted was for Kathleen to be with her!

Robert helped Elizabeth down the stairs, into the waiting car, and rushed her to Durban Hospital. She was immediately taken to the delivery room, where she labored for twelve grueling hours before finally delivering an eight-pound, five-ounce baby boy. He had a full head of black hair and didn't wait to be slapped on his rear before he started crying.

The doctor smiled as he said, "His lungs appear to be very healthy."

The next day, as Elizabeth tried to sit up in her hospital bed, the nurse brought her a tray of breakfast and the morning paper. She was famished and immediately dug into the plate of eggs and toast on her tray. As she took a sip of the coffee, she glanced at the paper and suddenly felt her heart race and cheeks flush, as what she saw paralyzed her. She was staring at a picture on the front page of the society section. It was Rex kissing a girl! The headline read "Rex Always Gets the Girl." She stared at it again, turned the paper over to check the date. This couldn't be right, but there it was right in front of her. She was stunned, frozen with the paper in her hand, her mind racing, searching for possible explanations, but the picture did not lie. No wonder he had not phoned her in the last several days! Elizabeth felt her heart beat faster, she could almost hear it. She wanted to cry, but she couldn't. Her face was now beet red, and her hands were shaking. For the first time in her life, Elizabeth Merrick Stewart was enraged.

Just then Kathleen walked into her room, mumbling something about Elizabeth and the baby staying with her until Rex came back.

Elizabeth took the newspaper and flung it at Kathleen and screamed, "Get out of here! Get out of this room immediately, and tell your son to stay away from me!"

"Elizabeth, dear, pay no attention to the newspaper article. There have been so many of these over the last few months. I just had the delivery man pull them from your paper so you wouldn't get upset."

"What? You mean you knew this sort of thing has been going on for months and no one told me?"

"It's just the way men are, especially in the cricket club. They get lonely when they are away."

Elizabeth felt like Kathleen was almost laughing at her, which infuriated her even further. "Get out! Get out of here this minute. I don't want to see you or anyone. *Get out!*" she screeched.

The nurses came running in and ushered Kathleen out of the room. They picked up the paper and couldn't help but notice the picture. They cleaned up Elizabeth's coffee and the food she had spilled when she was yelling at Kathleen. They tried to comfort the new mother, who just sobbed as her whole body shook. After a few hours, she had not stopped crying, so the doctor gave her a sedative and called for the baby to be given a bottle of formula since Elizabeth did not want to breast-feed.

Rex woke up in his hotel room with Joan, the young blonde he had met several months earlier, lying next to him. He had charmed his way into her bed, and she loved the publicity, while he loved the company when he was in England. She was beautiful and very sexy and so young. He couldn't wait to see her this time because, frankly, he couldn't stand to see what the pregnancy had done to his Elizabeth. He felt it made her unattractive, and he found he was unable to touch her. He was glad he was on the road and in England with Joan. He had woken up because the phone was ringing. It was his mother.

"Rex, I'm calling to let you know that Elizabeth had the baby yesterday. You have a son."

"What? It is too early. Is Elizabeth all right?"

"Yes, yes, she and the baby are both fine. They are at Durban Hospital."

"A son, I have a son, Mother. I have another week here, and I will be back in Durban the week after that. Please tell Elizabeth I will call her tonight."

"Yes, Rex, and congratulations, dear."

Kathleen chose not to tell him how upset Elizabeth was over the newspaper articles and photos. And she was glad he was not interrupting the test game to come home early. Maybe she would be rid of Elizabeth, after all, but she had to find a way to get her grandson.

After two days of Elizabeth crying and not eating, Dr. Barnes was worried. He'd seen postpartum depression before, but never this quickly or as acute. He asked the hospital psychiatrist, Dr. Jim Steel, to talk with her.

Dr. Steel entered Elizabeth's room just as she was throwing a newspaper across the room. He had to duck to avoid being hit. He immediately wondered if she was a violent person or just angry or depressed. He picked up the paper near his feet and laid it on the foot of her bed, then he sat on a nearby chair. He observed her for a moment as she fidgeted with her sheet and blanket. He was not sure if she was embarrassed or just a little nervous by his presence

Elizabeth wondered why this Dr. was in her room. She noticed his name tag read "Dr. Steel, Psychiatrist". *What did a psychiatrist want to see her about!* Of course, she realized it didn't help she practically hit him with her newspaper as he walked into her room. *How dare they send him to see her! What did any of them know of her situation.* She looked at him as he read her chart and noticed he was a handsome man with blond hair and very tanned skin. He had soft brown eyes and a strong jaw line. Finally, he closed the chart and spoke to her.

"How are you feeling today, Mrs. Stewart?"

"Don't call me that!"

"I'm sorry. Is the information I have on your chart incorrect?"

"No, I just want nothing more to do with that family."

Dr. Steel had heard of the Stewarts and could hardly blame the poor girl. He knew the Stewart's mother would do anything to advance her son's career and climb up the social ladder. "I hear you are not eating and you have not attempted to feed your baby."

"I'm just so mad—especially about the baby!"

"What are you so angry about?"

She pointed to the stacks of newspapers she had managed to gather thanks to the help of Mrs. Martin.

"Just look at all the papers! Articles and photos of my cheating husband! I came to this godforsaken place all the way from Perth, I miss my family, and my husband is a cad!" She started to cry again.

Dr. Steel handed her his handkerchief and said, "Why don't you call your family? Do they know what has happened?"

"Oh God! I hope not. I would be so embarrassed. Me with my big plans to travel the world!" She began to sob uncontrollably.

"I suggest you call your mother, Elizabeth. You need your family now." He remembered from her chart she was from Boora Rock. He picked up the telephone and asked for a line for a person-to-person call to the Merrick residence in Boora Rock.

Elizabeth's family knew what Rex had been up to. They had seen it in the papers there as well and assumed Elizabeth was trying to work out these problems on her own and save her marriage.

"Why don't you come home for a visit and bring the baby?" her mother said.

The minute Elizabeth heard her mother's voice, she began to feel calmer. She could almost see Bob Merrick's face at the suggestion of her coming home with a baby. Another mouth to feed, he would say.

"No thanks, Mom, I'll figure something out. Mom, I have not held the baby. I can't bring myself to…" More sobs.

"Elizabeth," her mother said sternly, "you must not take it out on an innocent child. He needs you."

Dr. Steel quietly left the room to give her some privacy as she spoke with her family. From the little he overheard, it did not sound like they were going to come to her rescue and he was disappointed to hear it. He hoped that in her state of mind and a with a new baby, they would get on a plane right away. Clearly she needed her parents right now, particularly, her mother. He worried about this young girl and wondered if he should do more for her. He was uncomfortable as he left her room.

After a long debate, her parents decided to send Abby to Durban to help Elizabeth. Abby had poured herself into her schoolwork after Elizabeth left and had graduated. She was ecstatic at the chance to go to Durban. They told her to pack immediately, and she would be there in a few days. Elizabeth's parents made it clear they wanted her to stay married to Rex, especially now that she had a child, regardless of his behavior. She had made a choice and a commitment, and they did not want any more scandal. They would send Abby to help her.

The next day Elizabeth heard her mother's words, *"He needs you,"* as she held her baby for the first time. She was feeding him a bottle the nurses had brought in. She just could not bear to breast-feed him. As she held him in her arms, she noticed he had her eyes and hair, and he had lots of it. She thought as she stared at the helpless little life in her arms she saw in him a resemblance to her mother, and that brought her comfort. She was glad the baby did not remind her of Rex.

Dr. Steel stopped in to check on her and was pleased she was calm enough to take care of her baby, but he worried about what the future would hold for the two of them.

Rex left Joan that morning with a lot on his mind, mostly a new son. He was happy at the thought of having a little Rex running about, but was completely dumbfounded on how to provide for him and Elizabeth. Now that there was a baby, Elizabeth would not be able to work, and the income from her job had been taking care of all the expenses back in Durban. He didn't think Elizabeth knew about the arrangement with the furniture store, or the new automobile he managed to get from the club, for that matter. In reality, Elizabeth had been supporting them.

Despite everything on his mind, Rex bowled great over the next two days. It was as if cricket saved him. He could immerse himself in the game and shut out the rest of the world. Nothing else mattered to him. The night after the last match finished, he was on a plane back to Johannesburg, where Robert would pick him up and drive him back to Durban. He was concerned that he had not been able to talk to Elizabeth since the baby was born. He could not reach her in the hospital or at the apartment. He assumed she must be busy with the baby and had taken the phone off the hook.

On Elizabeth's fifth day in the hospital, Abby walked into her room, and Elizabeth barely recognized her little sister. In the year and a half since Elizabeth had been gone, Abby had grown taller. Her hair was long and red. She wore makeup, and her figure had blossomed; her little sister had turned into a beautiful young woman. Elizabeth cried and hugged her sister. Abby was crying, too, and they kept hugging each other and crying before they ever said a word. The nurses all had tears in their eyes watching them, and they were grateful Elizabeth finally had family with her.

That afternoon Elizabeth and the baby were released from the hospital. She could not be released until she named the baby, but she couldn't come up with a name. All she knew was she did not want to name him Rex! So Abby named the baby Charles Rex Stewart, and they immediately began calling him Charlie. Mrs. Martin was kind enough to pick them all up at the hospital, and she had very generously loaded her car with groceries, diapers, baby formula, and everything else they would need. Elizabeth felt so grateful to Mrs. Martin and to Abby. After Mrs. Martin delivered them all to the apartment and said her good-byes, Abby made them dinner and helped Elizabeth give little Charlie his first bath. Then she fed him a bottle while Elizabeth took a shower and got comfortable in her robe and slippers. All the babysitting Abby had been doing over the years was coming in handy, and she was clearly more comfortable handling the newborn than her sister. Elizabeth was an emotional wreck and had no natural maternal instincts. She became flustered while changing his diaper, so Abby took over. She changed him and rocked him until he fell asleep and put him in his new crib. Then she made tea for the two of them. As they sat comfortably on the sofa in the living room, Elizabeth started to tell Abby all that had happened since she left home.

She told her sister about Kathleen and how she hated living in her house. She told her about Colin and Robert and her friends Miss Hunter and Mr. Stonely. She told her about the wedding and honeymoon and showed her pictures. She told her about her job with Mrs. Martin and the Indian market in Durban. She told her everything except what was happening with Rex.

When Abby finally asked her point-blank about Rex, she broke down again and said,

"Oh, Abby, you won't believe what he has been doing! I had no idea, and I feel like such a fool. And all the while I was setting up our home and carrying his child. How could he do this to me!"

"I am so sorry this has happened to you. What are you going to do?"

"I don't know. He should be home tomorrow. This should be such a happy time for us with our new baby, but I am so damned mad at him, and I really don't want to even look at him!"

On the long drive from Johannesburg to Durban, Robert asked Rex what had been going on with him while he was in England and mentioned what he had seen in the local papers.

"Oh no, please tell me Elizabeth has not seen them!"

"I honestly don't know if she has or not, but you might have thought of it beforehand," Robert said, a little disgusted with his older brother. He remembered taking Elizabeth to the hospital and how sad and frightened she seemed. He felt Rex should have been with his wife instead of frolicking around while he was away from home. It was late that night when Robert dropped his brother off in front of his apartment building. He felt no pity for him. He had made his bed.

Rex unlocked the door and walked into the living room to see Elizabeth and another woman he couldn't quite recognize.

"Hello, my beauty," he said as he crossed the room toward Elizabeth. She did not move from the sofa or run to him as she usually did.

"Hello, Rex," she said as she gave him her cheek. "You remember my sister, Abby. She's come to help me with the baby," she said coldly.

"Yes, yes, lovely to see you, Abby. It is very nice of you to come to help Elizabeth.

"Well, where is he? I want to see the baby," he said cheerfully.

Elizabeth got up from the sofa and took him into the nursery. There, surrounded in a cloud of blue, was this tiny creature with a head full of black hair, fast asleep. Elizabeth raised her fingers to her lips to motion to keep quiet and walked back into the living room, and Rex followed her.

"Well, he is a handsome young fellow, isn't he! Did everything go well, Elizabeth? Are you okay?"

"If you will excuse me," Abby said, "I'm going to take a shower."

Elizabeth watched her sister go into the bathroom and heard the water turn on, then looked to Rex with a stern face and said, "As if you really care how things went, you son of a bitch! How could you do this to us?"

"Oh, Elizabeth, I am sorry I couldn't be here when the baby came, I really am. Come on now, don't be upset. We have so much to be happy about, my beauty."

She reached down to the coffee table and spread out six different newspapers, all of which had been turned to the pages with him and Joan in the most recent three editions and other women in the first three. Then she sat back on the sofa and calmly said to him, "I would like you to stay with Kathleen, as I cannot bear to look at you. Abby is here to help me, and we will be fine. So please call a taxi to take you right away."

"You can't be serious, Elizabeth. Those women mean nothing to me. You are the only woman I love, and you know that."

"I will not be made a fool, and honestly, I cannot stand the sight of you right now. You must leave this apartment immediately," she said, and as she did, her voice rose to a level Rex had never heard before. Then the baby started to cry, and so did Elizabeth.

"Please leave now. I have to take care of the baby, and I cannot do it if you are here. Please just leave, now!"

Rex looked at the pain on Elizabeth's face and heard the baby crying. "Okay, I will leave for tonight, but I will be back tomorrow, and we will work this all out."

Elizabeth walked into the nursery to get the baby while Rex called the downtown taxi company, and within five minutes, he heard the cab horn honking outside. He stood alone in the middle of his living room, confused. Elizabeth was still in the nursery and Abby still in the bathroom taking what was the longest shower he thought anyone had ever taken. He picked up his bag and quietly let himself out.

Abby turned the water off and came out of the bathroom fully clothed the minute she heard the door shut and saw Elizabeth sitting in the rocker in the nursery, holding the baby close to her chest and crying.

Kathleen was surprised but happy when she saw Rex come into the house. "What are you doing here?" she said as she went to hug him.

"I wish I knew."

"What has happened? Is it Elizabeth?"

"No, Mother, it's me."

"Did you see her and the baby yet?"

"Yes, I did, but she didn't want to see me. In fact, she couldn't stand to look at me."

"She's upset over those newspaper photos, isn't she? I told her it was nothing, but she became quite rude

127

with me, really. She actually threw me out of her hospital room. She has some nerve, that one."

"Oh, Mother, please! She has every right to be angry with me. I just hope I can fix it."

He left his suitcase in the living room and walked down the street three blocks to the bar. He knew Colin would be there, and he could really use some cheering up. Colin was there in the big booth, and when he saw Rex come in, he got up and met him at the bar. He was surprised to see his brother since he hadn't been in the bar since he returned from England. And he did not look too good.

"So, how are you, you old bloke!" he said, patting Rex on the back. He motioned to the bartender to set them up with their usual.

"Did you know I am a father, Colin?" Rex said, not looking up from his drink as he gulped it down quickly.

Colin thought it best not to question his brother too much, based on his mood, he knew the best thing to do was let him drink and work through it.

"Well, that calls for another round, doesn't it!" he said as he motioned again for more drinks.

"Hey everyone, Rex Stewart has just become a father!" he yelled. Everyone in the bar yelled and cheered, and they all came to surround their favorite cricket player and shake his hand, and the drinks flowed.

Rex sat at the bar and felt like he was spiraling down to a place he did not want to be and he couldn't help himself. He was scared and afraid of the changes he thought had to happen now. He loved Elizabeth and was genuinely excited about his new son, but he had no idea what to do. He thought about it so much his head was pounding. He didn't know what to say to her or, worse, what to do with the baby. He didn't know how to fix it, and he didn't feel worthy of either one of them. He had truly believed once he was married he would settle down, and he did for a little while. Now, he wasn't sure if he could be faithful to one woman for the rest of his life. No matter how beautiful or special she was, he realized he could not do it.

So when the girl at the end of the bar smiled at him, he walked over to her and sat down and said, "What are you drinking, gorgeous?" He wanted to feel good about himself, and being with his teammates, women, and his friends was what made him feel good. Suddenly the team, Colin, and all of his local friends, many of them reporters, surrounded him and the beautiful girl named Monica. That was the last thing he remembered.

Elizabeth didn't sleep at all that night between her own crying and taking care of the crying baby. Abby offered to help in the middle of the night but Elizabeth knew she was tired from her long flight. Besides, she wasn't sleeping anyway. All of the dreams she once had with Rex were shattered and would never be the same again. She would never look at him or feel about him as she once had. She lay awake that night thinking she should forgive him and give him another chance, for the baby's sake, but the thought of him touching her after he had been with other women repulsed her. It also brought out her own insecurities about her sexuality and her ability to really satisfy a man or herself. She couldn't bear the thought of seeing the Stewarts, the press, or anyone remotely associated with cricket. She was ashamed, almost as if she had done something wrong. She also toyed with the idea that she should go back to Australia with the baby. But what kind of life could she and the baby have there? She thought about her brothers and knew she wanted more for her son. No, she would stay in Durban and keep a very low profile and raise her son. Mrs. Martin still wanted her to come back to work, and she would just make it work— somehow.

Abby woke up to the aroma of coffee that filled the small apartment. Elizabeth scrambled eggs and made toast for them, and as Abby watched her sister shuffle around the kitchen in her robe and slippers, she noticed how pale she was, and also how thin. You couldn't tell Elizabeth had just had a baby, as she was practically the same size as she was before the pregnancy. She had worked through her pregnancy, mostly on her feet, at the dress shop, and she clearly had experienced too much stress these last few days.

Abby was really worried about her because she was so pale and so very sad.

"This is delicious," Abby said. "I didn't realize I was so hungry."

Elizabeth nodded.

"Elizabeth, what can I do today that would be the most helpful? Shall I watch the baby so you can rest? Do you need anything from the market?"

"No, I don't need anything from the market, but there is something I would like you to do. Today's paper should be out on the stoop, and if you would look in the classified ads and help me find a babysitter? The quicker we set that up, I can go back to work, and you can go home."

Although Abby was not happy about the idea of going home so soon, she did as Elizabeth asked and went to get the paper. She brought it in and opened it up to find the classified section and left the rest on top of the dining table.

She was washing the dishes when she heard Elizabeth yell, "I cannot believe him!"

Abby looked, and on the front page of the sports section was Rex, surrounded by a group of men and a pretty girl, with his arm around her waist.

"I cannot believe he left here last night and went straightaway and did this! If he truly wanted to work this out, he would not be doing this again! Honestly!" Elizabeth got up from the table and headed toward the bathroom and slammed the door shut.

Abby read the article and realized Rex's brother Colin was with him in the picture. She remembered he was the brother Elizabeth was not particularly fond of, although Abby found him quite handsome. She didn't tell Elizabeth, but the story about Rex and his latest scores from the England game continued to another page, where another girl was kissing him. She put the classified section aside and threw the rest of the paper in the trash can, and then she threw the coffee grinds on top of it. She washed the coffeepot and the dishes, and when Elizabeth came out of the shower, she had a pencil and was circling some of the babysitting services that were listed. Elizabeth's eyes were red and her hair was wrapped in a towel. She was slamming doors and drawers as she was getting dressed, and Abby had never seen her sister so angry.

Rex woke up the next morning in an unfamiliar room with a familiar headache. He rolled over, and the girl from the night before was beside him, and he could not remember her name. She was naked, and he could smell the alcohol on her breath. He found himself looking at her and comparing her to Elizabeth. She was a pretty girl, but her hair was very fine, where Elizabeth's was thick. She had thin lips, and Elizabeth's were full and perfectly shaped. He wished he were lying next to Elizabeth and wondered if he could again. Seeing the girl start to stir, he slipped out of bed and quietly got dressed and let himself out of her apartment. Once on the street, it took him a minute to figure out where he was, which was only a few blocks from the bar. It was a clear and cool day, so he walked all the way back to Kathleen's house. He came in through the kitchen door, and Kathleen was sitting at the kitchen table.

"A telegram just arrived for you, dear. What can I make you for breakfast?" she asked, happy to have her favorite son at home.

"Bacon, eggs, and pancakes would be wonderful if it's not too much trouble, Mother," he said as he sat at the kitchen table and opened the telegram. It read:

DO NOT COME TO APARTMENT. NEWSPAPER
SPEAKS FOR YOU. ELIZABETH

Rex dropped the telegram and fumbled through the pages of the newspaper that were on the kitchen table. He found the picture of himself at the bar with the gang and the girl.

"Oh no," he said as he hung his head and rubbed his hands over his face. "I've really made a mess of it."

"What is it, dear?" Kathleen asked.

Rex pointed to the telegram and the newspaper. "I'm not hungry after all, Mother; I'll get something a little later." He got up and went upstairs.

Kathleen sat and read the telegram and looked at the newspaper article. She smiled, satisfied that her friends at

135

the press were doing a good job of keeping Rex in the limelight. She was even more pleased it was helping to get Elizabeth out of the picture. But her grandson! She wanted to see him and knew she had to make sure Rex did right by her first grandchild, with or without Elizabeth in the picture.

CHAPTER NINE

The weeks went by and turned into months. Abby had convinced Elizabeth to let her stay and help her with the baby while Elizabeth went back to work at the dress shop. Abby had secured a part-time job with a law firm downtown and coordinated her hours with Elizabeth's so that the baby was always with one of them. He was finally sleeping through the night, and he was growing every day. However, he was quite a fussy little baby. Elizabeth read in the papers that Rex was back in Australia and playing rather well, according to the test scores. She would read the papers and then throw them down with a "Humph."

Kathleen had come by one Sunday with gifts for the baby and asked to see him. Elizabeth reluctantly let her in, and she let her hold her grandson. She tried to talk about Rex, but Elizabeth would change the subject. She offered her tea and some shortbread Abby had made and tried her best to be as pleasant as possible. After about an hour, Kathleen asked as she was leaving if she could come back and visit him again. Elizabeth agreed, but asked that she please call ahead next time.

It was time for her postnatal checkup at the hospital, and as she entered the lobby, she ran into the handsome Dr. Steel, who stopped her.

"How are you Mrs. Stew—I mean, Elizabeth."

"I am fine. Thank you for asking, Doctor."

"And how is the baby?"

"He's just fine, growing bigger every day."

"You know, I've been reading the papers, and I understand you and Mr. Stewart are separated."

"Yes, yes, we are," Elizabeth said, offering no other information, feeling completely embarrassed.

Sensing her embarrassment, and feeling as if he had said too much, he offered, "If I can ever be of any help to you, or if you would like someone to talk to about it, I would be happy to offer my services."

"Oh, thank you, Dr. Steel, I appreciate that very much."

"Are you ill? Is that why you are here today?"

She smiled as she said, "No, not that I know of, I am just here for my checkup."

"Very good, well, I won't hold you up any longer. It was very nice to see you." He turned and walked down the long hallway.

Her checkup went well except that she was ten pounds lighter than she had been before she'd become pregnant. She was back on the elevator, going down to the lobby, when she ran into Dr. Steel again as the elevator stopped on the way down to a lower floor. They both smiled when they saw each other.

"This is a coincidence, isn't it?" he said.

Elizabeth smiled, but did not reply.

"I assume everything went well with your checkup because you look absolutely lovely today, Elizabeth."

She took a deep breath and said, "Thank you, but I don't feel that way at all."

"Elizabeth, you are a beautiful young woman with your whole life ahead of you."

She smiled and put her head down. He felt so sorry for this young girl and could see she was down on herself. He looked at her with her eyes down and blurted out, "I wonder if you would consider having dinner with me this evening?"

"Oh, I'm afraid I couldn't. I have to get home to the baby, and I have an early day at the dress shop tomorrow."

He chuckled. "All right. Well, please call me if you need anything. If you don't mind, I will call on you next week. Good-bye, Elizabeth." He got off the elevator in the lobby and walked down the same long hallway he had used earlier.

Dr. Steel was angry as he walked back to his office. He remembered what a difficult time she had when the baby was born, and he couldn't stand the thought of this beautiful young girl struggling alone with a baby, a job, and going through what she was with the likes of Rex Stewart. He was definitely going to keep an eye on her and the baby.

Elizabeth walked the eight blocks home feeling wonderful. She had been asked on a date, or had she? It had been such a long time since someone had paid attention to her, and she liked it. She was glad to know she was still attractive since she had Charlie. *Thank you, Dr. Steel, for making my day!*

It was the first time she felt any hope about her future since Charlie was born. Maybe she could find happiness without Rex, after all. Dr. Steel knew she had a baby, and he didn't seem to mind, and it didn't stop him from asking her to dinner. Was he going to ask her again next week? He said he was going to call on her, but maybe it was to just to check on her and the baby. She wasn't sure, but it didn't really matter because today she was feeling great.

She had not heard a word from Rex, and she really didn't care. So far she was managing, but she thought he at least should help her financially with the baby. Abby convinced her to see one of the attorneys at the law firm where she worked to discuss how to go about everything. She scheduled an appointment for Elizabeth to meet with the attorney at the firm who everyone joked about as being similar to a pit bull.

The following Wednesday afternoon, Elizabeth left work early to meet with William Adams at Canter, Morton, and Adams. Her goal was to get financial assistance from Rex to help raise their son, and nothing more.

William Adams, the youngest of the partners, slapped and rubbed his hands together with pure delight as he finished reading the fact sheet and newspaper articles Abby Merrick had given him for his next appointment, Elizabeth Stewart. How wonderful of Abby to bring this high-profile case right to him. The buzzer on his desk rang, and he heard Abby's voice saying, "Elizabeth Merrick is here to see you, Mr. Adams."

"Please bring her in."

His office door opened, and a beautiful young girl wearing a smart tan suit, with short brown hair, walked into his office. She was very different from Abby, taller, brunette, blue eyes, and absolutely gorgeous! He could see why Rex Stewart had fallen for her. He got up and shook her hand, saying, "How nice to meet you, Mrs. Stewart."

"Oh, please, just call me Elizabeth. I'm afraid the Stewart name is not one I'm comfortable with at the moment," she said rather nervously.

"For the purposes of these proceedings, you are going to have to get comfortable with the name. In fact, I suggest you embrace it for the time being. Now what, exactly, may I do for you, Mrs. Stewart?" he said as he raised his eyebrows at her and sat back in his chair, rolling his pencil between his fingers.

Abby had mentioned to Elizabeth that Mr. Adams was aggressive, but Elizabeth wasn't sure about his tone or his tactics as she sat before him. "I simply want financial assistance to help raise this child. And, I would prefer to have sole custody of him."

"Well, first things first. Tell me your story, and we will see what we can do," he said.

Elizabeth told him everything, from the first time she met Rex in Western Australia at the fashion show, until the day she asked him to leave the apartment. She would have preferred to keep some of his indiscretions quiet, but Abby had seen to it he had every newspaper clipping on his desk, starting with the first one of her and Rex. Elizabeth was very embarrassed that a complete stranger knew so much about her very private life.

She sat in the chair across from Mr. Adams, hearing only half of what he was saying. His sentences seemed clipped, but the one word she did hear that sounded in her ears was "divorce." A divorce! Somewhere in the back of her mind, she knew it would come to this, but she hadn't ever heard it out loud. She realized the marriage was over, and she knew she could never love Rex the way she had before. Mr. Adams was certainly being very direct with her, and after a few hours with him, she had come to appreciate his confidence. She watched him gesture with his hands to point or to make a fact, and he was still talking when she heard herself say, "Go ahead and file the papers."

Oh, what have I gotten myself into? She thought when the meeting concluded.

William Adams knew cricket players were at the mercy of their clubs. He also knew, in rare instances, if a player were very good, the sponsors would pay all their living expenses, including child support. Of course, these were arrangements all made very secretly and quietly. Lawyers would talk to each other without mentioning names, dates, or places, so Adams knew it was possible. He decided to leave this as a last resort and handle Elizabeth's case with the appropriate legal divorce papers containing custody and financial demands. In order to secure these for Elizabeth, he would have to take advantage of the press, but he could see this would be a problem for Elizabeth. Abby would be of assistance here, he was sure. In time, if she really wanted the money, she would come around on that issue. He would be patient with her, as he was really looking forward to the publicity for himself.

Kathleen sat in her parlor, drinking her tea and reading the Sunday edition of the paper. She turned to the sports section first, as she always did, and there she saw the article with a headline that read "STEWART'S WIFE

FILES FOR DIVORCE!" In reading the article, she noticed it also said Mrs. Stewart is seeking financial aid.

"That little witch," Kathleen said aloud as she slammed her teacup onto the saucer. She read on.

Mrs. Stewart's attorney, William Adams, was quoted saying, "Mrs. Stewart is very upset regarding the state of her marriage and her husband's behavior. She is requesting full custody and financial assistance for their only child."

"Custody! How utterly embarrassing. If it's the last thing I do, she will not get custody and try to keep me from my grandson," Kathleen proclaimed. She picked up the telephone and called Elizabeth.

"What do you think you are doing? Have you gone mad? You must contact the paper and have them retract this story immediately," she demanded.

"Hello, Kathleen, what are you talking about?" Elizabeth asked.

"Today's paper. Don't tell me you haven't seen it."

Mr. Adams had warned Elizabeth there would be an article in the paper about the divorce, and she had given him permission to quote her when he met with the reporters.

"Well, I haven't actually seen it, but I am aware of it. I think it is only right Rex should help to support our child," Elizabeth said confidently.

"Yes, well, he can't very well do that if you go off on your own, Elizabeth. If you really want financial assistance and help raising the boy, you need to move back to this house so the family can see to it the baby has everything he needs. You must stop this nonsense at once."

"I cannot and will not come back to that house. Rex was the one who broke the marriage vows, so he will have to figure something out. Good-bye, Kathleen." Her hands were shaking as she hung up the phone. "Well, it's done now," she said to herself.

CHAPTER TEN

For the past few months, Elizabeth had felt as though she was being followed. She didn't notice anyone in particular; she just had the strangest feeling all the time. It made her worry about the baby.

Dr. Steel had been calling her, and they had gone to dinner and a movie twice. Elizabeth felt very comfortable with him because he was very kind and he always asked about the baby. They were having dinner downtown at a new restaurant one night when a photographer snapped a photo of the two of them just as they toasted the baby's healthy six-month checkup. She wondered who would take a photograph of her when she was out on a date, and why. Was someone actually following her? She suspected the picture would also be in the sports section of the paper the next day, and she was concerned for Dr. Steel.

"Did someone just take our picture?" he asked, somewhat surprised.

"I'm afraid so. I think someone may be following me, and I've been feeling like that for quite some time now, although I can't imagine why, unless it has something to do with Rex."

"You are in the middle of a divorce from a well-known local hero."

"Yes, and don't I know it! But for heaven's sake, I am entitled to an evening out with a good friend," she said, taking a sip of her martini.

"Indeed you are," he said as he drank from his own martini and perused the menu.

Apparently, it didn't bother him in the least, and he was very supportive of her situation. She began to realize he wanted to know everything about her, just as she had once wanted to know everything about Rex. He knew when she was tired or had a bad day. He wanted to know all the daily details of her job at the dress shop and encouraged her to use her knowledge to obtain a better-paying job without ever making her feel inadequate in any way. Working at the dress shop was hard on her feet, and it was becoming boring.

A client at the law firm who owned a large travel agency had approached Abby. He was planning to open an office in Johannesburg and wanted someone with a winning smile and engaging personality to manage the office. He offered to double Abby's salary if she would relocate to Joburg. He also offered to find an apartment for her, pay the first three months of rent, and put all of these terms in a contract.

William Adams encouraged Abby to take the position, stating, "It would be foolish not to try it. What do you have to lose? We would reemploy you in a heartbeat should it be necessary."

So Abby accepted the offer and was to leave Durban within the month. Elizabeth would miss her terribly, as she had been such a huge help with the baby. She promised to send money to Elizabeth to help with babysitting costs in her absence, and she hoped Mrs. Martin would help her to find someone to watch Charlie. Maybe

Mr. Adams would get her some financial help so she would not have to rely on Abby for too long.

Oh, why do I have to worry about all this? Elizabeth asked herself. She was not happy at all, in fact, she was overwhelmed. Charlie was teething and woke her up at least twice every night. He was crawling early and was all over the apartment. She couldn't take her eyes off him for a minute. This last month without Abby there to help her had been exhausting. Simple things like cooking and showering had become challenging.

Elizabeth finally found a local woman to help with Charlie. She spoke English very well and was also Mrs. Martin's housekeeper, so Elizabeth felt safe leaving Charlie with her. Elizabeth's days were long and lonely. She hadn't heard from Rex, and she really did not care. Abby called her every Sunday morning, and during the week she worked at the dress shop and then came home and took care of Charlie. Her only contacts with other adults were Mrs. Martin and Abby's Sunday calls. She began to wonder what she was doing in Durban all by herself. She hadn't seen much of Dr. Steel since Abby left, as she didn't want to leave Charlie with a sitter after she had been gone all day at work, and she was worried about someone taking more pictures of the two of them. They decided to put things on hold until her divorce was final, but she realized during their brief time apart she really did not miss Jim Steel at all.

Abby wanted her to come to Johannesburg, saying her apartment was big enough for Elizabeth and Charlie. Abby was sure Elizabeth could easily find a job in the big city of Joburg. Elizabeth decided to talk to her attorney about taking Charlie and moving there so she could be closer to Abby.

Kathleen was worried about her grandson. She had not seen him in weeks. She was frustrated with Rex—what was he thinking! His wife had filed for divorce, custody of her grandson, and financial assistance. She had even heard through her sources Elizabeth was thinking of leaving Durban for Joburg because her sister had recently moved there. She had to stop her somehow, but needed Rex to help her. He had not been home in quite a while and was bowling better than ever, so she really could not expect him to do much now. She wrote Rex a letter asking him to try to do something about this dilemma with her grandson.

Rex received two letters: one from Elizabeth telling him she was moving within the week to Joburg, and one from his mother pleading with him to stop her. He had been in Salisbury, England, frustrated with the never-ending rains. He was due to return to Durban to play in all of Natal's six Currie Cup matches, and he was very excited about it. He knew Elizabeth and Charlie would be gone by then, and he decided not to stop Elizabeth from leaving, as he wanted her to do what she felt was best for herself and Charlie. He would have to fly through Joburg to get back to Durban, and he planned to pay her a visit then, giving her time to get settled in. He also decided to simply ignore his mother's request. He poured himself another cup of coffee and turned on the radio to listen to the latest scores of Athol Rowan, currently acknowledged as the world's best offspin bowler.

CHAPTER ELEVEN

Johannesburg, South Africa

1955

On a beautiful Saturday morning, Elizabeth got off the train in Joburg with Charlie in her arms and saw her sister, Abby, waving frantically to her with a porter in tow to help with her bags and boxes. She had packed everything in the apartment and left the furniture. She wrote Rex another note with her new address and told him to return the furniture. Abby took Charlie from her as Elizabeth directed the porter to ensure she had all her belongings.

It was a short drive to Abby's new apartment. It was on the first floor of a white, well-kept, three-story building on the corner of Kings Street and Smith Road. Being on the first floor, Abby had a screened back door that let out onto a nicely kept lawn with beautiful flowers and black wrought-iron tables and chairs. *Wonderful!* Elizabeth thought, *a place where Charlie can play and get some fresh air.*

154

They unpacked and settled Elizabeth and Charlie into the largest room in Abby's apartment, where she had already set up a crib. She had happily moved her things into the smaller bedroom, glad to have them both with her. Elizabeth had tears in her eyes as she hugged and thanked her sister.

By Sunday, Elizabeth had looked through the newspapers and circled a few classified ads in the employment section she thought she would inquire about. Abby had already taken care of interviewing and hiring a sitter for Charlie so Elizabeth could start looking and find work as soon as possible.

Elizabeth did find a job almost immediately, at Nestlé, as secretary to one of the vice presidents. He was a nice man who was married and had three children. He was very understanding and extremely patient with Elizabeth as she learned the office routine. Her typing was not the fastest, but he was happy to help out a young single mother. Elizabeth's divorce would be final within a few weeks despite Kathleen's attempts to make her move back to

Durban. No financial arrangement had been worked out yet, as Rex had hurt his shoulder and would not be playing for almost six months. Her attorney had suggested they try again for financial assistance once Rex actually had a paying job. So she was glad she found a job so quickly and was able to provide for herself and her son.

Charlie was growing and had taken his first steps at ten months old and you could not hold him back. Sally, the woman Abby had hired to watch him, was exhausted by the time Elizabeth came home from work every day. He was into absolutely everything—the pots and pans, Elizabeth's makeup, the garbage—and often would try to crawl out the screened back door, into the yard. He had to be watched every minute.

Abby was dating a South African man named Benny who was a sports coordinator for the Golf Association. He promoted golf tournaments and met a lot of people everywhere he went and made great friends. He was very jovial and pleasant and made people feel comfortable and at ease whenever he was around them. Elizabeth thought he was perfect for Abby.

One night Benny was having a cocktail party for some people he had met and been working with, and he asked Abby to come along and to bring Elizabeth too. He felt Elizabeth spent too much time alone and knew some of his friends would love to meet her. Sally agreed to watch Charlie for a few extra hours and a few extra dollars, which Benny insisted he would pay. Abby and Elizabeth arrived early to help Benny set up with ice they brought and the hors d'oeuvres they had made.

Guests were arriving steadily, mostly business people Benny and Abby had each met through work. Abby had invited David Williams, a marketing vice president from Horton Foods, one of the largest customers of her travel agency. She was David's travel coordinator and had helped made all of his travel arrangements through her agency. Benny had met David Williams a few times when he was in Joburg, and they got along great.

After a while, there were so many people in Benny's apartment, you could barely make your way to the refreshments. Elizabeth was trying to help by passing them around, and she looked at David Williams and asked, "Would you care for some nuts?"

He looked up, and this stunning brunette was holding a bowl of nuts out to him with a big smile on her face. She had the most beautiful blue eyes that seemed to bore into him and read his mind. She was slim and tall and had an accent he could not place, but he knew it was not Afrikaans or English.

"Why, yes, thank you. I don't believe I've met you. I'm David Williams." He held out his hand to take hers just as Elizabeth found herself being squeezed between two other people and steered slightly away from him.

"Hello, I'm Elizabeth, nice to meet you. Please help yourself," she said as she tried to extend the bowl to him.

He quickly plucked a few nuts as she struggled to hold it steady in the crowd. More people were gathering into the room, and it was getting loud. She turned to offer the nuts to someone else, and the crowd seemed to edge her even further away from him. Then Benny was there and started telling jokes to everyone, and they all roared with laughter.

Several hours and martinis later, Elizabeth was tipsy. She was having a great time and, in fact, had not laughed so much since she left Australia. The crowd had dwindled down to what appeared to be couples who had paired off, and Elizabeth was on the sofa, next to David Williams. They were laughing and making fun of everyone and their antics. David kept pouring martinis for them, and he apparently had had quite a few more than Elizabeth.

David loved hearing her laugh. It was the kind of laugh that made everyone in the room look at her to see what was so funny. Her smile was captivating, as was everything else about her. He wanted to know more about her, but was enjoying her company so much he did not want to talk about anything too serious.

Abby watched her sister that night and realized Benny was right—she did need to get out more. Abby

159

called Sally to check on Charlie, whom she said was sound asleep. She told her Elizabeth would be home in a while.

"Not a problem, ma'am, I'll stay as long as you like."

The drinks kept coming, and before Elizabeth realized it, she was kissing David Williams on the sofa. Just sweet kissing, no flirting, no explanations or expectations. Just holding each other and kissing. It seemed all right to Elizabeth, and it had been a very long time since she had been kissed. He was tender and courteous, never overstepping or rushing her in any way.

Elizabeth finally got hold of herself and slowly pulled away from him, and then she quickly stood up, embarrassed, and blurted out, "I have to go home—to my baby—right away!"

Everyone who was left in the room, David, Abby, and Benny, also jumped to their feet and scurried around.

"Yes, Elizabeth, right away—let's go," Abby said.

"Yes, of course," David said. "Can I give you a lift home?"

"No, no, David, old sport, I'll take the gals home," Benny said. "I'll see you soon."

And within what seemed like a minute, everyone was gone, literally leaving David outside on the stoop. He wasn't sure what had just happened, but he knew Elizabeth had a baby, and it didn't bother him at all. He wondered, as he started the short walk to his car and whistled to himself, if the baby was a boy or a girl.

The next day Elizabeth received two-dozen long-stemmed roses with a note from David, which read: *I was captivated the minute you offered me the nuts. Will you please do me the honor and have dinner with me tonight?* The note included his telephone number. She didn't have to think too long or hard about it. She had a great time, and she realized she wanted to get out more and have some fun. She was looking forward to being wined and dined, especially with someone so kind and handsome. She gladly dialed his number. It was a quick call and they agreed he would pick her up at 7:00 p.m.

Elizabeth worried all day about David knowing she had a baby, and she was mortified that she had just blurted it out last night after too many martinis. She wondered what he must think of her, already divorced with a baby. She also wondered what Abby and Benny had told him about her. She was tired of feeling guilty about her situation and Rex's poor behavior. She loved her little Charlie, and anyone who came into her life from now on would just have to accept that she was a package deal.

Abby and Benny came over that night to watch Charlie while she and David went to dinner. They brought a bottle of wine and a deck of cards to keep themselves busy.

David planned to take her to Kapitan's Oriental Restaurant on Kort Street, one of the oldest and nicest restaurants in Joburg. He called ahead and asked for a quiet table with a good view and asked for two bottles of their best champagne to be placed on ice. David was doing very well in his career working for Horton Foods as their international marketing vice president. He made a handsome salary and had traveled all over the globe. He had also managed to save most of his earnings, as the company covered his traveling expenses, and David always opted to be on the road, allowing his salary to go directly into savings for the past six years. He came from a stoic, hardworking Vermont family. He had three brothers and a younger sister whom he adored. He and his two older brothers all enlisted in the service during the war and had the good fortune to come home safely. His brothers had married and started families in the small town in Vermont where they were raised. David was very connected to his family and missed them all so much when he was away, but loved to come home and tell them of his travels and adventures. They would gather in his parents' living room and sip martinis while their Mom cooked huge family dinners and they laughed and shared each other's latest news.

David was really looking forward to his date with Elizabeth. He had been on many dates with women all over the world, but Elizabeth had a special quality that he couldn't quite identify. Whatever it was, he knew he just wanted to be near her. Her beauty was complemented by her elegance and kindness, and oh, what a laugh. When she tossed her head back and laughed, everyone in the room wanted to laugh along with her. He wanted to find out if this was the girl he had been dreaming about his whole life.

A chauffeur-driven limo arrived at Abby's apartment at 7:00 p.m. sharp. When Abby opened the door, a suited David Williams stood in the doorway with a silly grin on his face. Abby and Benny invited him in and offered him a cup of coffee, but he declined. Elizabeth had just finished zipping up the beautiful gold gown she had worn at the fashion show in Perth that felt like an eternity ago. She had shortened the hem and added pearls to the neckline. She slipped on the matching shoes, knowing she looked great. Elizabeth had grown more confident in her appearance and her abilities since her pageant days in Australia. She knew she was attractive and that she could support herself and the baby and had what she hoped would turn into a career at Nestlé. Riding in the limo with David

Williams, she felt wonderful for the first time in what seemed like ages. She was happy that she had been able to handle everything so far, but she was going to be more cautious in the future, and was determined not to make the same mistakes again.

The entire evening was perfect. David was a very attractive man who was well educated and accomplished. Unlike Rex, he asked Elizabeth many questions about her family, her past, and her hopes for the future for herself and her son. She was surprised she was able to be so open with him, even telling him how much her family back in Boora Rock embarrassed her. She told him everything about her brief relationship and marriage to Rex Stewart. David was so considerate and easy to talk to, and she felt very relaxed with him. She hoped he felt the same way about her.

David talked about his family. He told her they were more important to him than anything. He said he had hoped to marry, have children, and settle down in Brattleboro, Vermont, but the town was so small that his brothers had secured all the best jobs. They laughed together at this, as she could totally relate it to Boora Rock. He told her he knew he might have to continue to travel and hoped to find someone open to that idea, at least for the next few years.

That week they had dinner together three times, once with Abby and Benny, one night they went dancing after dinner, and once they met in the park for a late afternoon picnic, where David finally met Charlie, and he thought he was adorable. When he was at their apartment, Charlie teetered over to David and climbed onto his lap, obviously to get closer to the freshly baked chocolate cookies Elizabeth had set on the coffee table. David looked at Elizabeth, who nodded approval to give Charlie a cookie, and after that Charlie followed David everywhere, and David could not have been more pleased. He was used to being around kids because of his many nieces and nephews, and Elizabeth was happy to see David so at ease with Charlie.

What she did not know was David had been called back to the United States.

CHAPTER TWELVE

David Williams was in his hotel room reading, for the third time, the telegram he had just received. His mind was racing. The timing was all wrong for him to go back to the States. He had fallen in love with Elizabeth and knew he wanted to marry her, but he had hoped to give her more time to get used to the idea. He paced in his hotel room, thinking of everything—every detail, every situation, and every reaction that could come up if they were married. First, Elizabeth's reaction and, hopefully, acceptance of his proposal and his plan. He thought it through carefully, anticipating her potential worries with Charlie and working through each of them. Then he thought of Rex Stewart and the press, his own family, and the logistics to all of it. He knew he would have to be prepared if he were going to make this work.

He decided he would ask her tomorrow night, as tonight he was having dinner at Elizabeth's, just the two of them, and Charlie, of course. He wanted to enjoy one last night with her, just to be sure before he put his plan in motion.

Elizabeth was busily preparing a dinner for David of broiled lamb chops; she had become an expert at them by now. She laughed at herself as she recalled her first attempts to cook for Rex not so long ago. She also made asparagus, roasted potatoes, and custard for dessert. The table was set for two, as Charlie had already eaten and had his bath and was in his pajamas. Despite the tiring challenge of cooking and keeping Charlie on his schedule while she also got herself ready, she couldn't wait to see David.

He arrived on time, as always, with a beautiful bouquet of flowers for her, a bottle of wine for them, and a huge blue stuffed bear for Charlie, which Charlie immediately commandeered and began pushing around the apartment. Elizabeth noticed a slight nervousness about David and feared the worse—that he didn't want to see her anymore. Or maybe, he had met someone else who didn't already have a small child. But soon into the evening, his quiet, gentle manner had calmed her, and she was thoroughly enjoying his company. When Charlie's bedtime came, David offered to do the dishes and cleaned the entire kitchen while she put Charlie to sleep. When she quietly came back into the small living room, she sat next to David on the sofa. He lit cigarettes for the two of them, and they drank the bottle of wine and talked very late into the night. They held hands and had long, passionate kisses, and David realized it was time for him to go home. He told her he wanted to see her again the next evening, and she happily agreed.

For David's last night in Joburg, he planned a special night with Elizabeth. After the evening they had shared the night before, he knew without a doubt, he could not live without her and would propose to her that evening. He called Abby and told her his plan and she was thrilled for them.

Elizabeth was struggling to dress for her next date with David, and Charlie was getting into everything, as usual. He found her nail polish and started painting everything in sight.

"Oh, when will Abby arrive!" she cried to herself as she frantically retraced all of Charlie's steps with the nail polish remover.

She was not herself and was very sad since David had called her this morning and told her he had to go back to the States. He told her not to worry, that he would be back, but she was still really upset. She had come to love his quiet, gentle ways and strong character. Up to now, he had been a complete gentleman. Elizabeth secretly wished to take the relationship further, but knew it was impossible with him leaving.

Abby and Benny arrived to watch Charlie, and David showed up shortly thereafter with more flowers and this time a bottle of champagne. He asked Abby to get some glasses for all of them. Elizabeth noticed that same nervousness she had seen the day before and was worried. Her thoughts were racing as she watched him hoist Charlie over his head as Charlie squealed with delight. Was he going to toast to good friends and good times and walk out of her life? Abby came back in with the glasses on a tray, and Benny gladly poured for everyone. Then Elizabeth watched David stand up with his glass in hand as he spoke.

"Thanks to all of you"—and he looked directly at Elizabeth—"this past week has been one that has touched me deeply. I've made wonderful friends, and I've also met the most beautiful, fascinating woman and her sweet son." He tousled Charlie's hair as he said it.

Oh, here it comes, Elizabeth thought to herself, *the grand farewell!*

But David continued, "For many years now, I've been having a great time traveling the world and meeting people and making great friends, never really taking anything too seriously. Until now."

Elizabeth watched David and saw his face grow serious, almost somber, she thought. She watched him as he came closer to her, and she felt the warmth emanating from him. He placed his champagne glass on the coffee table and

171

bent down to her. *Oh my,* she thought to herself as her eyes grew wide, *he is going to propose!*

"Elizabeth you are the most amazing woman I have ever met. In addition to your beauty, you are intelligent, elegant, and pleasant. But mostly I see your kindness, Elizabeth, and I also see your pain."

At this, Elizabeth felt a lump in her throat and had to draw a deep breath.

"I promise you, I will never cause you the pain and disappointment you have experienced in the past. For the rest of my life, my focus will be on your well-being and your happiness, as well as little Charlie's. If you will allow it, I will raise him as my own. I know there is a lot to discuss and work through, and I promise you we will do so every step of the way together. Elizabeth, will you do me the honor of becoming my wife?"

Elizabeth looked at his handsome face and saw something she had never seen in Rex Stewart. A man capable of commitment. A promise from a man she liked and respected and knew she would grow to love even more.

She hesitated, and she wondered about the Stewarts, and little Charlie, and where they would live? A thousand questions were going through her mind.

David put his hand on hers and in a very soft voice said, "I will take care of everything, I promise."

That was all she needed to hear. "Yes, my darling, I would love to marry you!"

David pulled her up from the sofa, kissed her, and held her very, very, close. Abby and Benny were brimming with happiness for both of them. They all raised their glasses and toasted the couple-to-be. The four of them sat down and began to discuss how they could get Elizabeth and Charlie out of the country and away from the Stewarts, none of them realizing that today was also the day her divorce from Rex Stewart had been granted.

David gave Elizabeth his address and phone number in Vermont, his address and phone number for the office, and the name of his secretary who would know where he was and how to reach him at all times. He told her he would be back in a few months for her and Charlie. And then, as quickly as he had come into her life, he was leaving for the United States.

    Would he really come back? He had not given her an engagement ring, after all. The thoughts were swirling in her head. Along with her missing him so much, she could not focus on anything, not her job, not even Charlie, and she couldn't sleep. Thank God for her sister, Abby, she thought.

CHAPTER THIRTEEN

Rex Stewart woke up in an unfamiliar apartment in Durban. Someone was in the shower in the next room. He got out of the small bed and found his clothes and quickly put them on and left the apartment while the shower was still running. Once outside, he got his bearings and hailed a taxi to take him to Kathleen's house. When he entered through the back door of the kitchen, Kathleen was having her midmorning tea and reading the newspaper. She had a large envelope on the table that he could see had photographs sticking out of the edge. He poured himself a cup of tea and sat down.

Kathleen peered at him over her glasses and asked, "Did you know Elizabeth has been seeing an American man?"

"No, Mother, and frankly, I don't care. As long as she is happy and Charlie is well cared for, I really do not care."

"What if she tried to take him to America with this man? Then what will we do?"

"I doubt she would do that. He is my son, after all, isn't he?"

"Well, Rex, I've had someone keeping an eye on her."

"Yes, Mother," he said, exhausted with her constant interfering, "I can see that." He left the table and went up to take a shower.

Kathleen wanted to see her grandson. He was almost a year old now and probably walking and she didn't understand why Rex could not bring him over to visit her.

After Rex had his shower and a long nap, he came back downstairs for dinner. Kathleen started in again about wanting to see Charlie.

"I know Elizabeth is in Joburg with her sister, and it is only a six-hour car ride. Why can't you go and get him and let him stay here with us for a few days?"

He took a deep breath. As much as he would like to see Charlie, he wasn't sure how to go about it. He dreaded facing Elizabeth after he had abandoned her, and what would he do with Charlie once he had time with him? He supposed Kathleen would look after Charlie, but the whole idea was problematic for him. He ignored her pleas and began eating his dinner.

Waiting for a letter from David was draining every ounce of trust and courage Elizabeth had. It had been ten days and not a single word from him. She remembered Rex and his selfish cheating ways. She realized he never really took care of her or Charlie. She had been alone and that was not what she wanted. She tried to think of David who was a hard working man of character. She still felt alone and afraid, worried she would always be a divorced woman with a child.

"Who will want me?" she asked herself as she cried herself to sleep. She made it through her days and nights as if on automatic, just doing what she needed to do. But on the sixteenth day, a letter arrived from the United States, mailed from New York, and it was eight pages long.

"Oh, my darling," she cried, "you truly do love me!"

David's letter was full of his adoring love for her. He talked in detail of their future and the type of marriage he wanted. He told her he had started the process to bring her and Charlie to the States. Because of Rex Stewart and the press, he told her he would need Abby's help in getting her out of South Africa quietly. He didn't want any of that to complicate their plans. Abby helped him plan the trip by way of Rhodesia, and then Canada. Canada recognized other British Commonwealth passports, and Elizabeth's Australian passport qualified her for entry. He wanted to get them as close to him as he could. Entry to the United States would be more difficult, as a visa would be needed for both her and Charlie. An old college friend of his was practicing law in upstate New York, and he was willing to help with their visas. He also told her in his letter he had contacted a senator from Vermont in the hopes he would help expedite the whole process.

When she finished reading his letter, she was so relieved and happy. She took a deep breath and reread the entire letter over again. David was truly taking care of everything, just as he had promised. She had to be patient. She knew this process was going to take months. David said he would be back in South Africa in six weeks and they would discuss all the plans in more detail then. She found paper and pencil and began to write the first of what would become a lifetime of letters between the two of them.

CHAPTER FOURTEEN

Everything was going according to plan, and Elizabeth couldn't have been more pleased. Then one morning while she was a work, she received a phone call from Sally telling her Charlie would not wake up from his nap and had, in fact, been sleeping most of the day. She also told Elizabeth his breathing seemed labored and she found her empty sleeping pill bottle on the floor.

"Oh my God, call for an ambulance right away. I will be right there." She picked up her purse and told her boss as she ran by him on her way out she had an emergency at home. She ran the seven blocks to the apartment and saw the ambulance up ahead of her, parked outside the apartment building.

Her heart sank, and she prayed aloud, "Oh, please, I cannot lose my baby. Please help me!"

She raced up the steps, into the apartment, not noticing the bleeding blisters on her foot, and saw Charlie laying on the floor, pale, his eyes rolled up into his head.

180

The medics were on the floor taking his vitals, and then they picked up his little body and carried him out to the ambulance. As they passed by Elizabeth with Charlie, they told her he needed to have his stomach pumped. Her heart was beating so hard she almost fainted, but instead she followed them outside and climbed into the back of the ambulance with Charlie.

All she could do was look at Charlie's sweet little face and hold his hand. She was hoping he would open his eyes, but he didn't, and Elizabeth began to cry as she watched her little boy.

He was quickly admitted to the Johannesburg General Hospital. The nurses and staff paid special attention to Elizabeth and Charlie once they realized they were Rex Stewart's young ex-wife and son. One of the nurses knew Colin Stewart quite well and called him to ask if he knew about Rex's son being in the hospital.

They asked Elizabeth to stay in the waiting room while they pumped Charlie's stomach. While waiting there, she called Abby, and she was on her way.

The emergency room doctor came to speak to Elizabeth. "Charlie will be fine," he told her, "but it was a very close call. How did the child have access to those pills?" He asked her in a tone that made her feel guilty and nervous.

"They were in the nightstand, and Charlie has been getting into everything lately." She cried as she told him this. "I didn't think he would bother with them, though." By now Elizabeth was consumed with guilt and couldn't stop crying with concern for her sweet little boy.

The emergency room doctor sent for the new psychiatrist who had just transferred from Durban General Hospital. He heard he was very good, and he wanted him to talk to Elizabeth because she was so upset, but mostly he wanted his opinion on the stability of this young mother.

Charlie was resting comfortably in his hospital room, dozing in and out of sleep. Elizabeth was relieved he would be okay, but felt at fault for not realizing he might get into her nightstand. She sat by his bed, thinking of any and all medications or harmful products she would have to put up high or under lock and key. Abby had arrived at the hospital and was getting them both some tea.

Early that evening, Elizabeth was really taken back when a tanned Rex Stewart came into Charlie's room, and to make matters worse, Kathleen was with him. She was surprised they had driven up to Joburg. He was carrying a shopping bag, which he placed on the table at the foot of Charlie's bed. They both greeted her coldly and looked at Charlie, who had fallen asleep again.

"What have you done to this poor baby?" Kathleen asked.

Before Elizabeth could answer her accusing question, Rex added, "We heard about Charlie's accident and drove up as fast as we could; we have been very worried. How did this happen, Elizabeth?" He hated to ask this, and was himself consumed with guilt, as he thought leaving Elizabeth and Charlie on their own may have been too much for her.

"Obviously he got into some pills," Elizabeth answered, feeling quite defensive and annoyed. *How dare they even show up here?* she thought to herself.

Abby came into the room with the tea and heard Elizabeth's comment to Rex and his mother. "Perhaps you should talk in the waiting area, and I will sit with Charlie," she offered.

The three of them walked out of the room to the waiting area and stood there, each too uncomfortable to take a seat.

"Elizabeth, if you are not capable of taking care of my grandson, then let me take him home with me, and you can go on about your business with your American boyfriend!" she spat out. Rex said nothing, but looked down.

"I'm perfectly capable of taking care of my son. This was obviously an accident, one very awful incident that will not happen again."

"How can we believe what you say as we are standing here in the hospital with a very close call for that little boy?" Kathleen said.

Elizabeth wondered why Kathleen was doing all the talking.

"He has been just fine with me for over a year now," she said.

"Maybe it is too much for you, Elizabeth," Rex pleaded. "My mother and I would like to help care for the boy."

"Rex, I have custody of Charlie. He is in *my* care. This has all been settled with my lawyer, as you have been unable to provide for him."

"Yes, that is true, but my family has always been willing to help, particularly my mother, if you would allow it."

"No! Absolutely not! I have custody of Charlie, and I have been and will continue to take care of him."

"Well, that can change!" Kathleen said. "Maybe we should have the court revisit whether or not joint custody

185

may be more appropriate at this time!" She sat down in a huff, crossed her legs, and folded her arms over her chest, and Elizabeth knew she was going to be a problem. Rex walked back into Charlie's room.

Dr. Steel had been asked to come to pediatrics to talk to a young mother of a child who had just been admitted. As he was making his way to the child's room, he saw Elizabeth Stewart. *How wonderful!* he thought. Then he noticed Rex Stewart and an angry-looking older woman. He was surprised after talking to the doctor on call that Elizabeth was the woman they wanted him to speak to, but he was not surprised to see her having difficulty with her child or the Stewart family. He had always worried about her, remembering the difficulty she had bonding with the child when he was born. As he had come to know Elizabeth, he found her to be lovely, intelligent, and also a little on edge, and he always wondered about her emotional stability in dealing with what he knew was ahead for her as a single mother. *What a shame,* he thought to himself.

Dr. Steel approached Elizabeth and the angry woman. "Elizabeth, how are you? He noticed how distracted she seemed.

"Oh, hello, Dr. Steel, what are you doing here?" she asked clearly bewildered.

"I've just transferred to this hospital. I guess the more important question is why are you here, Elizabeth?"

"Charlie got into my sleeping pills, and they had to pump his stomach, but he is going to be all right. Thank goodness!"

"I'm glad to hear it. How are you holding up?" he asked.

"Well, I was just fine until Rex and his mother showed up." She tilted her head toward the angry woman who seemed to be listening intently to their conversation.

He noticed Elizabeth's eyes were darting everywhere, and she seemed a little disoriented or nervous. He was not sure which. "Why don't we go and have a look at Charlie?" He wanted to see how she was with him.

They went into the room, and he was awake again. Rex was showing him some toy airplanes he must have brought in the shopping bag. Charlie liked the planes, but was still very weak and just looked at them with a little smile. Elizabeth wondered if he even remembered who Rex was.

Rex stood up to introduce himself to the doctor. "I'm Rex Stewart, Charlie's father."

Elizabeth could feel her face get red with anger. How could he boast about being his father!

"I'm Dr. Steel, staff psychiatrist, nice to meet you." They shook hands.

"Hello, Charlie!" Dr. Steel approached the left side of Charlie's bed. "How are you feeling today?"

Charlie smiled and waved his hand, but was sleepy again. Rex excused himself, saying he would be back tomorrow. Dr. Steel sat on one side of the bed, and Elizabeth sat in a chair on the other side. She was very quiet, looking at Charlie. He assumed she was overwhelmed with concern for the boy, but he was disappointed when she started to tell him how angry she was and how much she hated Rex Stewart.

"Really, I can't stand him! How dare he even come here, and who does he think he is that he can just show up at any time, and especially now!" Her face was red, eyes darting, as she continued her tirade. "That son of a bitch! I don't want him anywhere near my child, and I am going to see to it that he won't be again!" she exclaimed.

"What do you mean, Elizabeth?" he asked.

"I have a plan to make sure he will not see him ever again. I will show him!"

By now her legs were crossed as she sat there, and her bloody foot was tapping rapidly in the air. Dr. Steel was concerned about her anger and resentment toward Rex Stewart, and didn't blame her, to a point. He didn't like that she was this vocal in front of Charlie, though.

"He is Charlie's father and does have some right to see him," he said, waiting to hear her response.

"He has no rights!" she almost screamed. "And I'm going to see to that, I promise you!" She was breathing

189

heavily and wringing her hands, and he noticed she was gritting her teeth with her last comment. He thought he should prescribe a sedative for her to help her calm down.

"Everything will be fine as soon as Charlie is better and you can take him home." He tried to assure her. "I will see you later," he said as he left the room to go the nurse's desk to order her a sedative.

Elizabeth was still sitting at Charlie's bedside when Abby came back into the room to be with her. Elizabeth watched him fall in and out of sleep for hours while she thought about her plans with David to take Charlie away. The nurse came in with a glass of water and a pill she said Dr. Steel wanted her to take this to help calm her nerves. He also sent in a salve for her blistered feet. He must have noticed them when she'd slipped off her shoes in Charlie's room. As she took the pill, she thought it was very thoughtful of him to think of her, and shortly afterward, she did start to calm down a bit.

Before Kathleen left the hospital with Rex, she spoke to the nurse who knew Colin and thanked her for calling the family. She was bragging about her son's cricket scores, and the nurse was hopeful Kathleen might introduce her to Rex next time he came in to visit Charlie. Kathleen really wanted to know what the medication was she had seen the nurse give to Elizabeth.

"I would very much like for you to meet Colin's older brother Rex. I think he is coming back to see his son tomorrow."

"Thank you, Mrs. Stewart. He is really handsome, and he is representing South Africa quite well!" the nurse said.

"Yes, I'm very proud of him. I'm concerned, though, that his ex-wife in there"—she looked at the door to Charlie's room—"will start making demands on him again. Honestly, she just will not let go of my son."

"She won't be bothering him for a little while now," the nurse said, "as the doctor gave her a sedative to calm her down. I guess she has been very upset about her son."

"Really?" Kathleen said. "She was that upset about it? Well, you could have fooled me. Knowing her, this

191

whole event was probably a big scheme to get Rex to come here to see her and that plan went terribly wrong!"

The nurse went about her duties, and Kathleen was satisfied she had information on Elizabeth that would help Rex's custody case. Elizabeth was clearly unstable! If Rex would not do something, then she would. She was determined to see her lawyer tomorrow and file for custody herself. This was exactly what she had been waiting for and she knew she must act quickly.

After spending the night at a nearby hotel in Joburg with Rex, and enduring the long ride back to Durban, Kathleen was tired and in a foul mood. When she was back at her home, she called her attorney, Dudley Stevens, and discussed the custody situation with him. He told her if they could prove Elizabeth was unable to care for the child, if they had a witness, and, most importantly, if Rex gave his approval, her chances of gaining custody as his grandmother were very probable. He would draw up the papers for her to sign tomorrow.

Two days later Charlie was well enough to go home. Elizabeth had to make sure he ate properly and was to bring him back in a week. Charlie cried as he was leaving the hospital because he liked all the nurses fussing over him, bringing him little gifts and all the ice cream he wanted. Elizabeth was happy to get him home and gave him some chocolate ice cream to calm him down. He was playing with the airplanes Rex had given him and was getting back to his happy self.

Kathleen left Dudley Stevens' office that morning feeling very pleased with herself. He had told her Elizabeth would be served with the custody papers late that afternoon. He also told her the nurse and Dr. Steel would be asked to testify on her behalf. She was concerned about Dr. Steel's testimony, as she remembered seeing a photo with him and Elizabeth having dinner some time ago. *All the better,* she thought to herself. *If he testifies for Elizabeth, I can say that he was another one of her many boyfriends. We still have the nurse who would be happy to help Rex Stewart!* She knew Rex would not be happy about any of this, but she was confident that he would go along with it after seeing Charlie in the hospital.

Elizabeth took a few days off from work to care for Charlie. She was thankful her boss was so understanding. She had just finished putting a chicken in the oven for dinner when there was a knock at the door. Charlie was still asleep from his afternoon nap, and she did not want him to wake up just yet.

She rushed to open the door, and a small man in a nice tan suit and hat asked, "Are you Elizabeth Stewart?"

"Yes," she answered cautiously, "who are you?"

"I'm from the Durban courthouse, and I'm here to serve you these documents," he said as he held out a large envelope to her.

"What are these about?"

"I don't know, ma'am. I just deliver them. Good day." He turned and left.

She thought these were probably papers David had sent to her, or something to do with their plans. She quickly tore open the envelope and was shocked to see she had to appear in court in Durban in two weeks because Kathleen wanted full custody of Charlie! She knew this woman had disliked her from the moment they met, but could not believe she would try to take Charlie. Where was Rex in all of this, she wondered?

Where was David? She called his office number in New York he had given her, but he was not in. His secretary took Elizabeth's name and number and said she would have him call her. David did call her late that evening. He was in Argentina doing market research for his company. He said he would try to come to South Africa for her court appearance, but he could not guarantee it, as his work schedule had him traveling nonstop. But, he promised to do his best to be there. He told her to call her attorney immediately to see what this was all about and that he would pay for his fees. Elizabeth did so the next day, calling the attorney she had used in Durban for her divorce, William Adams. When he called her back the next day, he had gone to the courthouse on her behalf, made a few phone calls, and had discovered they were going to try to say Elizabeth had neglected her son and that she was an unfit mother with emotional problems. He also told her it appeared this was Kathleen's case and that Rex had not been mentioned in it at all.

She was watching Charlie playing with the airplanes Rex had given him, running around the apartment with them in his hands like he was their wings, and she felt a tremendous weight suddenly pull on her chest. The thought of losing him made her heart ache. What would she do? Surely this had to be a mistake. Surely Rex would not allow this to happen! He wouldn't do this to her.

"Oh, David, I need you," she whispered to herself.

The next day she received a letter from David. One week after her court date was over, he wanted her and Charlie to start their journey to Canada. He was sure they would never take Charlie from her. He enclosed money for her bus tickets to Rhodesia, and a little extra for them to stay in a hotel there until the next leg of their journey, which would be a flight to London. He also told her how much he missed her.

David's letters were long and intimate, and her love for him was growing stronger every day. Knowing how deeply he loved her was giving her strength. Still, she was uneasy about giving up her job and her independence. Once again, she would be relying on a man to do the right thing and not only take care of her, but Charlie as well. She hoped David would live up to his promises. She did not want to be stranded in another strange country. However, as each of David's letters arrived—he was writing her daily now—the more she believed in the love they shared and David's commitment to her and to Charlie.

Elizabeth's lawyer in Durban, Mr. Adams, assured her over the phone the chances of her losing custody were unlikely, especially as she told him she had become friends with Dr. Steel in recent years. She planned her trip to Durban for her court appearance, and Abby and Benny were going with her to show support. Elizabeth called her old boss from the dress shop, Mrs. Martin, and she insisted they all stay with her, and she offered to watch Charlie while she was at the custody hearing.

The hearing was scheduled for 9:00 a.m. on Friday. Elizabeth had taken half a day off from work on Thursday, and all day on Friday, and Benny drove them all to Durban late Thursday afternoon. They arrived that evening at Mrs. Martin's, and she could not believe how much Charlie had grown. She prepared a wonderful dinner for them, and they all relaxed and caught up on the local Durban gossip.

The next morning, after an early breakfast, Elizabeth, Abby, and Benny headed to the courthouse. Before they even reached the steps to enter the building, cameras were everywhere. Reporters crowded around Elizabeth, one asking "Why haven't you taken care of your child?" and another asked, "Do you believe you are a good mother?"

Benny and Mr. Adams were practically pushing them out of her way as they entered the courtroom. Kathleen had done a good job of spreading the word about her case. Reporters and photographers were not allowed inside, and the noise came to an eerie halt as the doors closed behind them and Elizabeth took her seat. Kathleen sat opposite her, with her attorney and with a haughty look on her face. Elizabeth ignored her. The judge came in, both attorneys approached the bench, and then Kathleen's attorney, Dudley Stevens, spoke first.

"We are here today to challenge the sole custody of Elizabeth Stewart in regard to the minor child, Charles Rex Stewart, age one. We will show the court that Elizabeth Stewart is simply not capable to continue to care for this child. Our first witness is Nurse Rita Andrews, who works at Johannesburg General Hospital."

"Miss Andrews, can you tell us how you met Mrs. Stewart?"

"I met her when her son was admitted to Joburg General Hospital for an overdose."

Someone seated in the courtroom gasped.

Mr. Stevens continued, "And what was the boy's condition?"

"His breathing was labored, he was in a semi coma, and his stomach had to be pumped."

"And how did Mrs. Stewart appear to you?"

"She was upset. I remember she had severe mood swings—one minute crying, the next very angry—so much so the doctor ordered her a sedative to calm her down."

"Was Mrs. Stewart admitted to the hospital as well?"

"No, but the doctor treating her son asked our staff psychiatrist evaluate her."

"I see. Thank you very much, Miss Andrews."

Then Elizabeth's attorney, Mr. Adams, approached the nurse to ask a few questions. "Miss Andrews, do you know what the boy overdosed on?"

"No, I do not."

"Do you know how or when he ingested the medications?"

"No, I do not," she answered, a little embarrassed.

"Do you know if he was ever admitted to the hospital before this incident?"

"No, he was not."

"And how do you know that?"

"We would have had a file on him, and we always check the files when a patient is admitted."

"And the child was fine when he was discharged?"

"Yes, he was."

"Do you know who the child's father is?"

"Oh yes," she answered gleefully, "he is Rex Stewart."

"And did you speak with Mr. Stewart?"

"Yes, his mother introduced me to him at the hospital the second day Charlie was in the hospital."

"Oh, so you know Mrs. *Kathleen* Stewart?"

"Well, we got to know one another at the hospital, and she is a very nice woman."

"Did you 'get to know' Mrs. *Elizabeth* Stewart at the hospital?"

"No, I did not."

"And have you gotten to know the famous Rex Stewart?"

She blushed as she answered, "Well, actually, yes, I have. We had drinks together when he was in Joburg those few days."

"I see," said Mr. Adams. "Thank you, Miss Andrews."

Elizabeth felt Mr. Adams did a good job of exposing the nurse as another cricket fan of Rex's. Next, Kathleen's attorney called Dr. Steel. Elizabeth was relieved when she saw him approach the bench to take his oath. She couldn't believe the nurse and Dr. Steel had been summoned and had to travel to Durban to testify. Of course, she couldn't believe she had had the good luck of running into him at Joburg General and had been surprised when he told her he had transferred there from Durban.

Dudley Stevens started questioning him. "Dr. Steel, when did you first meet Mrs. Elizabeth Stewart?"

"I met her over a year ago, when I was practicing at Durban General Hospital, when she delivered her son."

"Was she a patient of yours back then?" he asked, somewhat surprised at the possibility.

"Um, yes, she was," he seemed embarrassed to say.

Delighted, Mr. Stevens pressed on. "Why were you treating Mrs. Stewart at that time?"

Dr. Steel sighed before he answered, "She had a severe case of postpartum depression."

Oh no, Elizabeth thought to herself, *he won't have to go into all that! Hopefully he won't make it sound too serious.*

"So you are saying, Dr. Steel, as a psychiatrist that Mrs. Stewart had emotional problems at the time the child was born?"

"Um, yes, but there were very difficult circumstances for a woman who had just delivered a baby," he said, trying to defend Elizabeth.

"I understand that you are practicing at Joburg General now and coincidentally had to be called in as psychiatrist again for Mrs. Stewart during the child's hospital stay. Is that correct?"

"Yes," Dr. Steel replied.

"And how did you find Mrs. Stewart this time?"

203

"She was very distraught and very angry," he said quietly.

"Angry?" Dudley Stevens questioned. "Angry with herself for neglecting the boy?"

"No, she was very angry with Rex Stewart and his mother," Dr. Steel answered.

"Why was that?"

"She felt they were interfering and was upset they showed up at the hospital to see the boy."

"So," Dudley Stevens pushed, "the grandmother and father of the child drive six hours out of concern for the child, and she is so angry about this they have to call in a psychiatrist who has to give her a sedative to calm her down?" he asked, sounding astonished.

"Yes, that is what happened," Dr. Steel answered quietly.

"Would you say, Doctor, that Mrs. Stewart is unstable? And, please remember, you are still under oath."

Dr. Steel felt cornered. In the time since he first met Elizabeth, he had thought her reactions were a bit excessive, even though she had endured a lot of challenges. He had to be honest. As much as he wanted to protect Elizabeth, he could not lie under oath.

"I believe under normal circumstances and the right environment, Elizabeth Stewart would be fine," he answered, proud of himself.

"So, you are saying any challenges or stresses she may encounter would cause her to have a highly emotional reaction?"

Elizabeth was surprised at the direction the questions were going, and also at Dr. Steel's responses. She knew he was remembering Charlie's birth, and her reaction to Rex at the hospital, and her darned bloody feet. *Oh, what a mess I've made,* she thought to herself.

"In some circumstances, yes," Dr. Steel finally answered. "It is my professional opinion she would benefit from psychiatric treatment and medications to keep her calm during those times."

"Thank you, Dr. Steel. That will be all."

Elizabeth was very embarrassed, and Abby was spitting mad. She felt they had not talked about everything Elizabeth had endured over the past year—trying to raise a child on her own and work full-time, dealing with Rex's abandonment and Kathleen Stewart! She wanted to wring Dudley Stevens' neck, and Dr. Steel's as well.

Then they questioned Kathleen and called several character witnesses on her behalf. To Elizabeth's horror, they produced a letter from Rex stating he supported his mother having custody, as it would allow him, as the boy's father, to assist in raising the boy. *There it is,* Elizabeth thought. *He has disappointed me once again.*

The judge called for a recess to make his decision. Elizabeth could not believe this was happening. How could they take her son from her? This just could not be happening! Abby, Benny, and Mr. Adams were trying to be supportive and keep her calm. Abby was disappointed in Mr. Adams, as he had not called any character witnesses for Elizabeth, and she pleaded with him to at least let her and Benny speak on Elizabeth's behalf.

"It is too late, I'm afraid." He hung his head.

Abby wondered if Kathleen had somehow put pressure on him. After a few hours of waiting on the decision, she decided to get them some food, worried Elizabeth had not eaten very much in the past few days. Abby felt better as she did get Elizabeth to eat half a sandwich and a cup of tea just before the court clerk called them back into the courtroom. When everyone was seated, the judge, looking very solemn, began to speak.

"Custody matters are never easy to resolve. It tears at one's heart to even consider removing a child from its mother's care. I have decided in this case, based on the witness testimony, medical records, and the letter from the child's father, that the minor, Charles Rex Stewart, would receive the proper care and attention in the custody of his grandmother, Kathleen Stewart. He would also have the benefit of his father and the entire Stewart family. Therefore, Elizabeth Stewart, you are hereby ordered to bring the child to Durban one week from today, next

Friday, to the home of Kathleen Stewart, where he shall reside indefinitely.

Kathleen and her cohorts were full of hugs and cheers for each other as the judge left the room.

Mr. Adams turned to Elizabeth and said, "I am so very sorry." He packed up his papers and left the courtroom.

Stunned, Elizabeth, Abby, and Benny remained in their seats. Benny said, "What has just happened?"

Elizabeth felt dizzy and could not speak.

Abby stood up, taking Elizabeth's elbow. "Come on, Elizabeth, let's go."

Elizabeth tried to stand up, but her legs were unsteady. She fell back in her seat.

Abby and Benny each took an elbow as Abby said again, "Come on, let's get out of here."

They managed to get her out of the building, where the reporters were waiting with their cameras flashing. "How do you feel about losing your son?" one asked.

Abby could not believe they could be so cruel. Benny was trying to keep them at bay as they made their way to the car.

"Do you feel Rex Stewart will be a good father to your son?" another asked.

With that question, Elizabeth began to cry. They made it to the car, where photos were taken of Elizabeth in the backseat, covering her face with her white gloves and sobbing.

Benny drove around for a while before going back to Mrs. Martin's. He wanted to give Elizabeth time to collect herself before she saw Charlie. He felt terrible for her, and he believed an injustice had been done.

Elizabeth sat in the car, thinking of Charlie and feeling like she had failed him. She had worked so hard to provide for him this last year. She could not imagine Kathleen taking better care of him or loving him the way she did. She worried Kathleen would take her dislike for her out on Charlie. And Rex! What could he possibly teach Charlie? The thought of Charlie living with them made her physically ill. She said aloud, "What will I do without my baby?" and stared ahead as the tears rolled down her face.

Abby said, "Don't worry, Elizabeth. We are going to straighten this mess out very quickly. And, I think we should call David as soon as possible."

"David!" Elizabeth cried. "What will he think?"

"He will not think any less of you. I can tell you that for sure," Benny said.

"I won't let them have him," Elizabeth said. "Over my dead body. I will not let them take my Charlie!" She finally stopped crying, and now she was getting mad. She was supposed to leave with Charlie next Friday on the bus to Rhodesia, and she was still going to do so, she told herself. She sat in the car, planning their escape out of South Africa. She knew it would be especially dangerous right now with all the political turmoil going on, but she had to keep Charlie away from the Stewarts. She did not mention any of this to Abby or Benny, and when they were back at Mrs. Martin's, she hugged Charlie and held him very close and did not want to let go of him.

CHAPTER FIFTEEN

At breakfast the next morning, Kathleen was reading the paper and noticed a photo of Charlie with Rex and Elizabeth when he was first born, and beside it a second photo of Elizabeth in the backseat of a car, crying.

"Good!" she said. "She was nothing but trouble for my son!"

Rex finally woke up and came down for lunch and saw the paper his mother left on the table. His heart sank. "Oh, my poor Elizabeth," he said aloud, "I never meant to hurt you. I never should have let Mother talk me into signing that damned letter."

Kathleen entered the kitchen talking loudly about which bedroom she would turn into a nursery for Charlie and trying to decide which of the servants would be his nanny and what school he should attend when he was old enough.

"Do you think he will be as good a cricketer as you are, dear?" she asked Rex

211

"What about Elizabeth, Mother? She does not deserve this. What have we done?" He felt awful about it because he knew the best place for Charlie was with Elizabeth.

"She was nothing but trouble from the minute I met her, and Charlie should be with us," Kathleen said. "Don't worry about her. She will be just fine."

Disgusted with his mother, Rex got up from the table and called Colin to go have a drink with him at the pub.

While they were at Mrs. Martin's house to pick up Charlie and their bags, Mrs. Martin, Abby, and Benny made a great fuss over Elizabeth and Charlie. She had stopped crying and was still holding on to Charlie. They finally said their good-byes to Mrs. Martin, and they climbed back into the car for the return trip to Joburg. Abby was worried, as Elizabeth was very quiet during the ride home. She didn't want to talk about it and just held Charlie close as he slept in her lap.

Later that evening, when she was home and had put Charlie to bed, she called David. She sobbed as she told him and could barely get the words out.

"I've lost my baby, and I feel like I just want to die," she cried to David. "I cannot let them take my baby from me. I just can't."

"Oh, darling," David said, "I'm so sorry to hear all of this. We will find a way to work this out, I promise you. I am so sorry I wasn't there, but we are going to get through this. No one is going to take you or Charlie away from me!"

His words made her feel better, and she told him she still wanted to get on the bus next Friday and go to Rhodesia as they had planned. She did not care if they came after her or if she were a fugitive; she could not, and would not, give Charlie to anyone! David wanted her to remain calm, and he told her he would call his friend the attorney, and possibly the senator, to see what could be done. The next day he called her again.

"Elizabeth, I'm very concerned about you taking the bus to Rhodesia. The authorities have raised bus fares, and there are protests, and, in fact, a bus boycott. It will be very, very dangerous to travel cross-country right now," he said.

"I have to get out of Joburg right away, David, as I am sure Kathleen is having me followed again."

"All right, my darling, I do understand. But can you really do this, Elizabeth?"

"Yes, David, but I am so afraid. I know I need to follow the court decision, but I have to save my child. Yes, I have to do it, and I can do it," she said bravely.

"All right, but you should not tell anyone, except Abby and Benny, as we are going to need their help. By the time you are in Salisbury, I will have your airfare and more money waiting for you there so you can fly to London. I will take care of everything, Elizabeth. I promise."

She felt so much better and knew it was her only option. David helping her made her believe it could be done.

Midweek she told Abby and Benny of her plan. They were afraid for her, but said they would help however they could. Elizabeth had packed her old red suitcase on Wednesday. She took only a few items of clothing for herself and Charlie, and a few toys. She needed to pack light so she would be able to handle the suitcase and Charlie, and by Thursday morning she was ready. She had decided to go into work as usual that day. She would just not show up on Friday. She could not risk telling anyone of her intentions or even resigning. She hated not telling her boss, as he had been so kind and patient with her, but she could not risk jeopardizing her plan. She would ask Abby to pick up her last paycheck. Maybe someday she would be able to write her boss and apologize for her hasty departure.

When she came home from work that evening, Abby and Benny had let Sally go home early; they could not risk telling her either. They simply told her to take Friday off, with no mention of Monday's schedule at all, as they knew someone would question Sally. Abby prepared a nice dinner for them as they talked through their plans and any potential obstacles they might encounter.

CHAPTER SIXTEEN

The next morning Abby and Benny drove them to the bus station. Elizabeth was terribly sad to say good-bye to Abby and was not sure when or if she would ever see her sister again. It was a tearful farewell for the two sisters, but they knew they had to protect Charlie. Once they were on the bus leaving Joburg, Elizabeth was quite nervous, as she was aware of the locals boycotting the buses in Rhodesia. She hoped she would be safe on the bus, but feared there might be protests as they neared Salisbury. She had read in the papers they had blocked a bus on the road, and the police had a difficult time controlling the boycotters. She tried not to think about all of that, as she was determined to get Charlie to safety and away from the Stewart family.

She realized it would be a long twelve-hour ride north. They would make stops along the way as other passengers got on and off, and hopefully, there would be no trouble at any of the stops. Again, she tried not to think about the danger and to focus on Charlie and their future

217

with David. She gave Charlie half a chicken sandwich, which she broke into very small pieces for him, and a drink of milk from a small thermos she had packed. He was excited to be on a bus and stood on the seat, looking out the window and playing with his airplanes.

It was a bumpy and dusty ride, and after five hours, they stopped in Makhado. Elizabeth was relieved to find the bus station clean and quiet; she felt they would be safe here. She washed up and changed Charlie, and she bought them a Coca-Cola, which thrilled Charlie, as the bubbles made him laugh, and he would let it drool out of his mouth. After thirty minutes for the passengers to stretch their legs, they boarded the bus for the next leg of their journey. More passengers boarded the bus than were on before. They were all either English or Afrikaans, and Elizabeth thought this unusual and wondered why there were not any locals on the bus. She sat looking at the other passengers and wondered where they were going. She worried someone would recognize her as Rex's wife and became uncomfortable when she overheard someone several rows behind her talk of a cricket match he planned to attend in Salisbury.

Oh no, Elizabeth thought. *Please don't let Rex be there!* If he were there, that would mean reporters would not be far behind him. Many of them were friends of Kathleen's, and she would never get Charlie out of the country unnoticed! Again, she forced herself not to worry about it just then and to try to think positively. She thought of David and how much she loved him and how wonderful he was to help her and Charlie. She was very excited to begin her new life with him. He was going to try to meet them in London for a few days, and she couldn't wait to see him again.

After a few more hours and several stops, they crossed the border into Rhodesia. She still had five more hours on the bus before they would arrive in Salisbury, where she would stay for a couple of days to rest up before flying out for London. It was getting late and she fed Charlie the rest of the pieces of the chicken sandwich, and a banana. She was too nervous to eat anything.

A few hours later, she awoke to loud voices, while Charlie was asleep in her arms. The bus was traveling through an extremely large crowd that was apparently protesting the increased fares, just as David had warned. She saw their hand-painted signs and their angry faces. She noticed a few uneasy policemen trying to keep them off the road. The bus had slowed down and was inching through the crowd as they grudgingly let the bus pass. Elizabeth felt like it was a sea of people who slowly backed off the road ahead as the policemen pointed their guns at them. Charlie was awake and wanted to stand on the seat and look out the window, but she held him back. She heard loud thuds as some of the protestors threw rocks at the back of the bus as it passed them. When they were finally about to get past the crowd, a rock smashed through the rear window, hitting a man in the eye. He was bleeding, and passengers started screaming for help from the bus driver, who ignored their pleas, as he was focused on getting past this mob as quick he could. A few minutes passed, and all was quiet again. A passenger tended to the man's eye and said he was hit on the brow and it didn't appear to be too serious.

Finally, at eight thirty that evening, the bus pulled into the Salisbury depot, where the tired and haggard passengers disembarked. Elizabeth and Charlie were in the middle of the group, trying to stay inconspicuous.

Fortunately, there were porters there to help with luggage, and taxis lined up on the gravel road. Elizabeth saw her red suitcase and asked one of the porters to take it to a taxi for her, and she followed behind him with Charlie still asleep in her arms. She struggled to get a rand out of her purse to give the porter. Once they were in the taxi, she told the driver to take her to the Meikles Hotel, where David had reserved a room for her. Elizabeth was on edge, exhausted, and afraid as the taxi drove through the dark streets. She was very aware of her vulnerability, a woman traveling alone with a small child late at night in a strange city and she wondered if the driver might not be taking her to the hotel, but she tried to think positive and prayed she and Charlie were in good hands. *Oh, David,* she thought, *I*

221

miss you, and I am so tired and afraid. She looked out the window and saw signs and advertisements for the cricket match for the coming weekend and knew she would have to be very careful not to be noticed. As the taxi pulled up to the hotel, Charlie woke up crying.

"We're here, Charlie. We are at a very nice hotel with a nice bed for you," she said cheerily. "Let's go inside and get out of these dusty clothes." She very quickly paid the driver and walked inside the hotel lobby.

David had registered her under Abby's name, and Abby had given Elizabeth her identification papers. They could take not take any chance of Elizabeth being recognized before she left for London.

"Will you be needing a crib for the boy, Miss Merrick?" the clerk asked her.

"No, thank you," she said. She wanted to be close to Charlie tonight and would just use pillows to keep him safe in her bed. She knew he must be exhausted and confused and was afraid this trip might have been too much for him. She wanted him to feel safe. A porter came to carry her suitcase to their room, and she gave him a rand after he unlocked the room and gave her the key.

It was a beautiful room with a sofa and two chairs, a large desk so she could write to David, and a separate room with two beds. She quickly ordered a snack for the two of them from room service and gave Charlie a bath. The cookies and milk for Charlie and the steak and beer for her was exactly what they needed. Charlie fell asleep quickly, and Elizabeth took a long, hot bath with the door open to listen for Charlie, then finally crawled under the crisp, clean sheets of her bed.

"Thank you, my darling David," she said out loud just before she fell asleep.

The next morning, Charlie woke her up saying, "Mama, Mama." She got out of bed and changed his diaper. Then she let him teeter around the hotel room as she ordered a huge breakfast for them both and turned on the radio.

As she looked out from her third-floor window, she could see in the daylight what she had not been able to see the night before. There were banners and posters everywhere for the upcoming cricket match. Some of them even had photographs of the players on them. She did not notice Rex on the ones she could see from her window, but decided to stay in her room all day and not take any chances of being recognized.

However, by five o'clock that afternoon, Charlie was climbing the walls, and so was she. She decided to take Charlie on the elevator down to the lobby and out to the gardens for a little while. He had lost interest in his airplanes and was chasing a small ball she had packed around the grassy park. As she sat on a bench watching Charlie play, she could see through the glass doors of the hotel, into the lobby, and that is when she saw John Macheeth, Rex's sponsor. She quickly snatched Charlie into her arms and went around the side of the building, hoping to find another door so she could get back to her room unnoticed. She managed to find the staircase, and ran up it with Charlie in her arms, and closed her door behind her as she gasped for air. Charlie was crying, as she scared him when she scooped him up so abruptly and ran with him, leaving his ball behind.

"It's all right, my sweetie," she said. "Mummy will get you another ball; we just had to come inside very quickly." She held him close and stroked his head as he calmed down. Then she ordered dinner for them, and from the nearby Sundry Shop she ordered him a small new ball and a peroxide hair-dye kit for herself.

As John Macheeth finished his martini in the lobby lounge, he wondered if it could have been Elizabeth Stewart he had just seen in the garden. He was pretty sure it was her, as he would never forget her beautiful legs. If it was her, he wondered, what was she doing in Salisbury alone with a toddler? He knew traveling was very dangerous right now. He also knew the Stewart's were divorced and in a custody battle but Rex had not talked about his wife and child in months so he was not sure exactly what the situation was now.

He would ask Rex when he saw him later and give him a piece of his mind for allowing her to come to Salisbury

225

under the current conditions. What a bastard Rex could be, he thought to himself as he ordered another dry martini.

"Twenty-four more hours," Elizabeth said to herself as she washed and hung Charlie's diapers to dry around the room in preparation of the next leg of their trip. She had been rinsing his soiled diapers at the bus depots and keeping them wrapped tightly in waterproof bags until she got to the hotel. David had understood she would need a few days after the bus ride with Charlie to prepare before she was ready to board the plane for London.

David called her that morning and told her the plane tickets and money for the London flight should be delivered to the local travel agency that afternoon. She couldn't wait to see him again. She thought how lucky she was to have met someone who was so willing to help her raise Charlie. Several hours later, the phone rang, and the desk clerk told her there was a telegram for her at the front desk. She knew it was from Western Union and that David had sent the money for London.

The next morning she went down to the lobby to find out where the nearest Western Union office was and to hire transportation to get there; fortunately the hotel had a car that took her and Charlie. She had dyed her hair blonde the night before, so she was not quite as nervous about going out in public and being recognized. Next, she went to the travel agency to pick up her tickets for the flight. On the way back to the hotel, she had the driver stop at a restaurant, where she ordered lunch for herself and Charlie. *Just a few more hours,* she thought to herself, *and Charlie, David, and I will be together again.*

At the lobby bar in the Meikles Hotel, John Macheeth was asking Rex about his wife. It was difficult to understand him, as he had arrived only a few hours ago for tomorrow's match, but he was already on his fourth martini.

"So what is the story with that beautiful wife of yours?" he started.

"My wife?" Rex responded as he stared into his glass. "I wouldn't know at the moment."

227

"Oh, I see," Macheeth responded, more confused.

"Yes, you see," Rex went on, "I seriously doubt she would bother with me again, as my beautiful wife is no longer my wife." He gulped his martini and waved to the bartender to bring him another.

Macheeth felt sorry for Rex. He should be on top of the world right now, as he was batting seventy-five and was at the top of his game. He couldn't help but wonder why he chose to drink and womanize instead of taking advantage of this opportunity to succeed. Still, he was sure he had seen his wife yesterday, but given Rex's mood, he decided to mind his own business and not mention it now. He left the bar and went up to his room to call his own wife.

Rex stayed at the lobby bar and flirted with two very young English girls who had managed to sneak away from their family. As he spoke with them, he would glance up at the mirrored wall behind the bar. He suddenly saw a small boy who looked about Charlie's age, and his heart ached. He watched him in the mirror, kicking a ball in the park outside the lobby entrance. He stared intently, and the more he looked, he could have sworn it was Charlie, but it had been a few weeks since he'd last seen his son, and this boy was much steadier on his feet. He swiveled on the barstool to get a better look at him and was convinced it was his son, but the woman with him, sitting on a bench with her head down, reading something, was plainly dressed and had platinum blonde hair. He shook his head and told himself his mind was playing tricks on him, and he swiveled back around in his seat to order another drink and lit up a cigarette.

Elizabeth kept her head down, afraid to look up. She had seen him at the bar with the two young girls. She knew there was the side entrance to the stairs she had found the other day. She kept her head down, telling Charlie to stay close to her. Finally, she glanced up, still keeping her head down, and saw he had turned back around. She quickly lifted Charlie and his ball and walked quietly to the side entry. Back safely in her room, with Charlie taking his nap, Elizabeth paced the floor. If she had not had David's letter in her hand at the moment she saw Rex, she knew she could not have remained as calm as she did. Now, all she had to do in the morning was get out of the hotel and to the airport, unnoticed. She called down to the gift shop and ordered Charlie the hunter's khaki-colored outfit she had seen in the window, which came with a large hat. She also ordered herself a pair of oversized sunglasses. She thought about dressing Charlie in a girl's outfit, but decided against it.

The next morning, after breakfast, all packed and ready, she and Charlie took the elevator down with the bellman and walked out the lobby doors to a waiting taxi. They slipped into the car and drove off, and Elizabeth sat back in her seat, removed her sunglasses, and breathed a sigh of relief and smiled. She had done it, and right under his nose! The confidence that came over her only increased her confidence and her desire to see David.

CHAPTER SEVENTEEN

Elizabeth had given Charlie one-quarter of a crushed sleeping pill in his milk, so he slept for most of the twelve-hour flight to London. She could not risk him making noise and drawing attention to them on this flight. When he woke, he was hungry and wet, and after she cleaned him up, they ordered a snack on the plane, which he thought was great fun as he played with the tray table. He stood and looked out the window as Elizabeth handed him his toy airplanes.

David was waiting at Heathrow Airport. He hoped they would be on the plane when it landed. He was so worried for the both of them and knew they still had a long battle ahead of them. When he wasn't working, he was talking to his lawyers and the senator from Vermont about their next steps. They assured him once Elizabeth and Charlie were in Canada, they would be safe from South African courts. The next challenge would be to bring them into the United States. He tried to place a long-distance call to the airport in Rhodesia to see if they had indeed boarded the plane, but he could not get through. He had spoken to Elizabeth the night before and knew Rex was staying at her hotel for the cricket match. He couldn't believe the bad luck she was having on this trip and could only hope Rex had not recognized her and tried to stop her, or worse, tried to take Charlie from her.

He tried to imagine what she would look like with her blonde hair, although it really didn't matter, as he loved her and couldn't wait to see her and Charlie. He had bought a double-decker toy bus for Charlie and had it with him, as well as an engagement ring for Elizabeth.

The plane landed, and passengers deplaned onto the tarmac. It was raining, and he stood in the rain under his umbrella, waiting for them. It was cold, as it was November, and he hoped they had warm clothes with them. He finally saw her and thought she looked like a movie star, blonde hair and still wearing the sunglasses. She looked tired and a little disheveled carrying Charlie, a small diaper bag, and her purse. She was even more beautiful

232

than he remembered, and he kind of liked the blonde hair. He ran to the bottom step and covered the three of them with his umbrella. He took Charlie and hugged him, and he took Elizabeth into his arms, and he kissed her. She laughed, and her eyes filled with tears as she hugged him again. They realized they were blocking the way for the other passengers and still had to find her luggage. She spotted the red suitcase, and David picked it up, not waiting for a porter. The three of them huddled under the umbrella and made their way to a waiting taxi for their trip to the Dorchester Hotel.

David had reserved a two-bedroom suite for them. He also hired a babysitter for when Charlie went to bed around 7:30 p.m. He had ordered Elizabeth a new cocktail dress and shoes. She was a perfect size-six dress, and he had called Abby about her shoe size. He had reserved a table in the dining room and ordered a bottle of their best champagne. He wanted to propose, officially, tonight and give her the ring. He assumed she and Charlie would take one of the bedrooms and he the other. He did not want to make her uncomfortable with him in the same suite. They had one week together in London before they all flew to Canada. He had taken time off from work and wanted to spend every minute with them both. Charlie was a sweet and happy little boy, and he was looking forward to getting even closer to him.

At dinner, Elizabeth began to relax. They were finally with David, and they were safe. She loved London and was looking forward to doing some sightseeing and, hopefully, shopping in this sophisticated city.

The restaurant was beautiful, the service was excellent, and the food was delicious. David reached across the table for her hand as he said, "I have missed you so much, and I was hoping we would be able to spend some time like this together."

"Oh, my darling," she said, "I feel like I am in a wonderful dream."

"Good! That is exactly what I want for you and for Charlie—always."

234

He pulled the sparkling ring from his pocket and slipped it on her finger, and as he did, he said, "I want to marry you as soon as possible. Let's get married here in London."

Her eyes filled with tears, and she said, "It really is a dream, isn't it! Yes, yes, my darling, I can't wait to be your wife."

"I am so very happy, Elizabeth." For the first time in his life, David Williams fought back his own tears.

Elizabeth looked at the big, sparkling ring on her finger and noticed how truly beautiful it was. She immediately was concerned about David's finances and all of the money he had spent on her and Charlie already.

"This ring is absolutely stunning, my darling, but can we afford it?" she asked quietly.

"Yes, we can. Do not worry. As I told you before, I make a very good salary and have saved my earnings for most of my life. Now, with you and Charlie, I have someone to share it with."

And so it was settled. The next afternoon, David and Elizabeth were married in a registrar's office in London. Elizabeth had purchased a simple cream-colored suit with matching hat that had a small mesh veil. David dressed in a black suit, and to her delight, he had taken Charlie with him while she was shopping for her dress and bought Charlie a suit that matched his own nearly exactly. She thought they were adorable.

Back in Durban, Kathleen was livid when Elizabeth did not show up with Charlie on the court-appointed date. She had been calling her for days, and her sister would only tell her Elizabeth had left their apartment and was on her way to Kathleen's with Charlie the last time she had seen her. Rubbish! Kathleen did not believe her for one minute and knew the two sisters where in cahoots. She called her attorney, who then had the authorities go to Elizabeth's apartment, and the sister gave them the same story. She then called Rex and asked for his help, but he really did not want to force this issue and worried perhaps something may have happened to Charlie and Elizabeth while traveling from Joburg to Durban. He tried to convince Kathleen of this possibility, but she simply did not believe it. She knew Elizabeth would rather die than give Charlie to her.

After two weeks, Kathleen's attorney successfully had Elizabeth charged with kidnapping, so she called her friends at the police department to make sure the warrant had been issued for Elizabeth's arrest. Then she called her friends at the press and had them all over for high tea. She gave them the entire story, complete with photographs of Elizabeth and Charlie. She had current pictures of Charlie that she managed to take when he was in the hospital while Elizabeth was busy meeting with the psychiatrist. She had managed to hide her camera from Elizabeth in a very large tote.

The next morning, it was in all of the South African newspapers. Rex was mortified by his mother's actions and wanted her to just leave Elizabeth alone. He knew she would take good care of Charlie and believed the best thing for him to do was to leave them be. He wished his mother would see that, for his sake.

Mr. and Mrs. David Williams were enjoying London and their honeymoon. They took Charlie to Big Ben, Buckingham Palace, and the River Thames. Eventually they hired a nanny which gave them more time to have wonderful romantic dinners followed by dancing or long walks along the Thames. David was such a loving man, always thinking of Elizabeth's feelings and needs. He made her feel like she was the most important thing in his life, and she really was. David was just as happy as Elizabeth and felt she treated him the same way.

Their week in London was nearing an end, and they were finalizing their plans for their stay in Montreal. It was only a five-hour car ride from there to Brattleboro, Vermont, David's hometown. The plan was to leave Elizabeth and Charlie in Montreal until the paperwork for their entry into the United States was finalized, and he would drive up every weekend to be with them.

David went down to the hotel lobby early one morning to buy cigarettes for himself and some chocolates for Elizabeth. While in the newsstand area, he noticed the *Cape Times*, a South African newspaper, with a small picture of Elizabeth and Charlie on the front page. "Rex Stewart's Wife Kidnaps Son" was the headline. David did a double take and stared at it in disbelief. He picked up a paper, leaving money on the counter, and quickly hurried to a private spot in the lobby, pulling the paper apart to find the entire article.

Oh God, he thought to himself, *what have we done!* He was worried for Elizabeth and for an instant wondered what he had involved himself with. But, he immediately dismissed those thoughts and tried to focus on how to deal with the situation while keeping Elizabeth and Charlie safe. He ordered himself some coffee, took a seat, and thought about what could be done. He realized the farther away they were from South Africa, the better, and he had to get Elizabeth to the United States as soon as possible. Once in Canada, he would work harder to get her into the States. He had been formulating a plan to deal with the Stewarts that he hoped would be agreeable to Rex Stewart, in particular. He also thought it best if he did not share this information with Elizabeth. She had already been through too much.

On their last day in London, they relaxed by taking a leisurely walk with Charlie and stopped off at a park along the way. They discovered Charlie loved fish and chips, so that was what they had for lunch quite often. David was trying to keep the newspapers out of Elizabeth's sight. He had decided if he could prevent it, she would never know the South African authorities were after her.

CHAPTER EIGHTEEN

Montreal was very cold, and Elizabeth hated it there. It was December, and there was snow and ice everywhere. The air was so cold, it hurt Elizabeth's lungs as she breathed. Charlie had become accustomed to the bitter cold, and David seemed to revel in it. He would wear turtleneck shirts with wool sweaters and corduroy pants. Elizabeth and Charlie didn't own anything so heavy, so their first task was to buy warmer clothes.

David had to go back to work the day after they arrived and he had rented a cozy two-bedroom apartment for them on a monthly basis. He did not know how long it would take to bring them across the border, and he wanted them to be as comfortable as possible.

David's job required him to travel extensively, and although he lived in Brattleboro with his family, he would receive his assignments by telephone or mail, and he would fly out of Boston Airport and stay on location for several weeks or months, which, of course, was how he had met Elizabeth. He had been inquiring within his company for

241

positions that would allow him to stay in one place for longer periods of time, as he was getting concerned about being gone so much with a new wife and child. He was not having much success.

Meanwhile, David's attorney was working on the visas for entry into the United States. This would require a background check, and fortunately, Kathleen's attorney had filed the arrest warrant with the Natal authorities, but not the federal authorities.

Elizabeth hated the scratchy high-neck sweaters she had bought for herself. And no matter how many pairs of socks she wore over her stockings, her toes were still cold in her snow boots when she went out. She was also frustrated at the time it took to put Charlie into his snow pants, jackets, boots, gloves, scarf, and hat just so they could venture to the market. Charlie was adjusting to the cold and sliding along the sidewalks and playing with the snow, while Elizabeth struggled with the groceries, the icy walkways, and her ugly boots. She hated her boots and missed her high heels. She felt fat in all of the sweaters, coats, and scarves and she hated how the hats ruined her hairdo. Charlie liked to play in the snow and had seen some children making snowmen at a park near their apartment. To get them both some fresh air and out of the cramped apartment, she would take Charlie to the park every afternoon, where they would try to make a bigger snowman than the day before. Sometimes while Charlie played in the snow, Elizabeth would sit on a bench under an umbrella so the snow would not fall on her, and she couldn't understand why passersby looked at her and chuckled. She had long decided she did not like the snow, ice, and bitter cold.

David's first weekend back in Vermont, he drove to Montreal on Friday afternoon and arrived at 8:00 p.m., just in time to see Charlie before he went to bed. Afterward, Elizabeth and David were so happy to see each other, they made love and stayed up most of the night talking about the week's events and the status of their plan to get them to Vermont.

David's attorney had been making progress with the Vermont senator, who assured them he would sign a personal letter of recommendation for Elizabeth's visa when it came across his desk. The visitor visa process could take six to twelve weeks, and David was a little worried about Elizabeth's dislike of the cold weather, particularly, when he explained winters in Vermont were also cold and snowy.

Elizabeth came out of the bathroom pulling the wool sweater away from her neck. "These things are just awful!" she cried.

"What is the matter, my darling?" David asked.

"It's the clothes you have to wear here. They are ugly, heavy, and they itch like the dickens!"

"Maybe you should buy something with a different material?"

"Well, I bought what the store had on display and on sale," she said with an edge in her voice.

"Perhaps you should look for some cashmere or velvet. It is much more comfortable," he offered.

"I will do that straightaway, as I can't stand these things!" she said again as she pulled the gray, itchy sweater away from her neck.

Then David told her he was trying to get a more permanent position in a warmer climate, and she was thrilled. "I don't mean to complain, my honey, but I do believe I am better suited for a bit warmer climate. Thank you for trying to arrange that." She sat next to him on the sofa, calmer now as they snuggled to keep warm, and later in the day, he took her shopping for some softer warm clothing.

What he did not tell her was the offer he and his attorney had airmailed to Rex Stewart. They sent the documents to the Natal Transvaal cricket team, marked "personal and confidential" in the hopes it would reach Rex directly and would not be seen by Kathleen.

After weeks in the cold Canadian weather, Elizabeth was in a foul mood. And to make matters worse, she slipped on the ice one day walking to the corner grocery store and sprained her wrist. Her groceries scattered on the sidewalk as she fell right on her rear end, breaking her fall with her right arm and worrying Charlie would run into the road.

"Damn this blasted ice!" she cried as she quickly picked up her groceries with Charlie in one arm and the grocery bag in the other.

When she got back to the apartment, she called a doctor, who came over and put her arm in a sling.

After that she found she became frustrated easily with sweaters, coats, and boots for Charlie and herself, and she missed David terribly. Some weekends he could not come to see her, as he was traveling in Argentina and Mexico on assignment.

"Sure! He is nice and warm, and he's left us to freeze!" she told herself. Then she felt terribly guilty thinking of all David was doing for her and Charlie. At least she could try to remain positive.

CHAPTER NINETEEN

It was Valentine's Day weekend and David was driving to Montreal Friday morning, hoping to arrive around noon. He was very happy, as Elizabeth's visitor's visa had finally been approved, and he was going to bring Elizabeth and Charlie home to Brattleboro with him on Sunday to meet his family. They would stay with them until he found something more permanent within his company, where he did not have to travel so much and they could come with him. He had initially been a little worried how his family would feel about him marrying a divorced woman with a small child, so he made a point of speaking to his parents first to get their approval to bring them home, and then he sought out each of his three brothers and his sister to ask them all individually how they felt about it. To his delight, they were all very supportive and happy for him and were looking forward to meeting this intriguing woman their brother had secretly married.

When he arrived, he found Elizabeth in an arm sling and miserable.

"Oh, David, I am so glad you are here," she said as she ran to him and flung her one good arm around his neck.

Charlie followed her lead and hugged David around his legs. If he had had any doubts, their reception made him even more confident about his plans.

"Let's pack your suitcases," he said to Charlie and lifted him up and threw him in the air.

"Why, are we going on a little trip tomorrow?" Elizabeth gave him a confused look.

"Yes, we are. We are going to Vermont tomorrow," he said, with an adoring smile as he played with Charlie.

"Have our visas come through?"

"They sure have," he said as he reached for the envelope in his coat pocket.

"Oh, darling, we can finally leave this iceberg!" Elizabeth cried and hugged David while Charlie was still in his arms.

They packed, and the next morning they ate a big breakfast, trying to use up the food in the apartment. They were leaving with only their suitcases, as the apartment they rented had come completely furnished. Elizabeth dressed in a smart, navy blue suit and dressed Charlie in the suit David had bought him for their wedding. She realized she would be meeting her new mother-in-law and prayed it would be better than it had been with Kathleen. She was also nervous about meeting David's large family and felt a twinge of sadness at how much she missed her sister, Abby.

They arrived at David's home in Brattleboro at 3:00 p.m., and it was quite a full house. She met David's brothers Jeff, Mike, and Jim, and their wives, who were all very friendly. She met his little sister, Pamela, whom she felt an immediate connection with. And, she loved his mother the minute she took Elizabeth into her arms and welcomed her to the family with a big hug and a bright smile and asked her if she was hungry.

Then she picked up Charlie and told him how handsome he was in his suit and that she adored his British-

249

sounding accent as she handed him a fresh-baked cookie. Anna Williams could see immediately why her son was so enchanted with them both.

There were children everywhere! David had neglected to tell her that his brothers were all married and they each had two or three children under the age of five. Elizabeth was delighted that Charlie finally had someone to play with. They were all very kind and polite, and the adults talked and laughed as they enjoyed martinis before dinner. Elizabeth felt very much at home and smiled at David across the room. He winked at her, and they held their martini glasses up to each other in a silent toast. Elizabeth sat back on the very comfortable sofa, taking in her surroundings, and she felt she finally belonged.

A few weeks later, Elizabeth realized how deeply she cared for the Williams family. Her mother-in-law, Anna Williams, was strict but kind, and was clearly the family matriarch. She taught her family the value of hard work, kindness, and respect, and they returned it in kind. Anna taught Elizabeth to cook and, in particular, to bake.

Elizabeth discovered she loved being in the kitchen with Anna making large family meals and, under Anna's guidance, fabulous desserts.

Still in Rhodesia, Rex Stewart was handed a large manila envelope that had been mailed from the United States. He couldn't imagine what it was about as he sat down in his hotel room that morning recovering from a wicked night of drinking and a raging headache. He took another sip of coffee and pulled out what appeared to be legal documents. He read the first paragraph of a letter, and it immediately grabbed his attention.

Dear Mr. Stewart:

I am writing to you at the request of my client, David Williams, husband of Elizabeth Stewart Williams.

Mr. and Mrs. Williams request that you persuade Kathleen Stewart to relinquish custody of the minor child, Charles Rex Stewart, and have all charges against Elizabeth Stewart withdrawn.

Furthermore, we believe if you can, yourself, obtain custody of the minor child, you could then surrender him to the care of Elizabeth Stewart Williams.

Additionally, Mr. Williams would like to adopt the minor child and has agreed to raise the child as his own and provide for him as necessary until he becomes an adult without any interference from you. Obviously, this would relieve you of any further financial responsibility to the minor child.

Lastly, Mr. and Mrs. Williams request you have no contact with them or the minor child whatsoever and that all communications be handled through this office. I may be reached at....

Rex finished reading and calmly put the papers down and drank another sip of coffee. He wasn't sure if he was jealous or angry. Who was this David Williams, he asked himself. His mother had warned him about the American Elizabeth was dating, but he couldn't believe she was already married to him. He noticed the envelope was mailed from New York, but the lawyer was from a place called Vermont. Where were Elizabeth and Charlie? His mind was racing from anger and jealousy to concern for

Elizabeth and his son. Why hadn't he at least stayed in touch and helped her? He was fraught with guilt and regrets. What could he do now? Was it too late? He decided he needed to absorb all of this and think about it. He also decided he would not share any of this with Kathleen, as that would only complicate matters, and he needed time to figure out what to do and how to respond.

After a shower and a big lunch, Rex went down to the lobby of his hotel in Salisbury. He looked into the mirror behind the bar and realized this was the same hotel where he thought he had seen his son a few months ago. Going over it in his mind, things were starting to make sense. Elizabeth had never shown up with Charlie at his mother's house in Durban when she was supposed to, and she was nowhere to be found. And those ridiculous kidnapping charges his mother had brought about—he was still not speaking to her. However, Elizabeth did take his son, God only knows where, and she had remarried. He never doubted she would take good care of Charlie, but he could not believe she had actually taken off with him to avoid giving him to his mother. Quite frankly, he couldn't blame her. But the courage Elizabeth had shown in taking the boy, he didn't know she had it in her. Another wave of regret and guilt overcame him.

As Rex drank away the rest of the evening, that regret and guilt turned into anger and selfishness. Why should he agree to those absurd requests from this David Williams fellow? Who did this chap think he was anyway?

By then, John Macheeth had joined Rex, and as usual, his friend was whining about his failed marriage. Only this time, John noticed he seemed a bit angry as he relayed the latest news to him. As he listened, John realized it must have been Elizabeth Stewart he had seen a few months ago.

"You know, I think I saw her right here in this hotel," he confessed to Rex.

"Is this your idea of a joke?"

"No, I really thought I saw her in the park out there. Sorry to say, old chap, I could never forget her beautiful long legs."

"I thought I saw my son out there a few months ago, too, but the woman with him was blonde, and…Oh my God."

They looked at each other realizing it had been Elizabeth and Charlie.

"Why didn't you tell me?" Rex asked.

"You were so drunk and depressed and I decided not to mention it to you. Sorry, old chap," he said as he stared down at his drink.

Rex drank so much that night he passed out at the bar. His teammates carried him to his room. They were all getting annoyed with his excessive drinking, as it was starting to affect his game and his scores.

After two weeks of this behavior, his teammates urged him to make a decision and move on. He decided to comply with all of Elizabeth's husband's requests, with a few conditions of his own. He felt he deserved something out of this arrangement as well. After all, as he remembered, as much as he had loved Elizabeth, he felt their marriage had been an arrangement that simply did not work out. He placed a call to David William's attorney, John Gregory.

"This is Rex Stewart calling from South Africa for Mr. John Gregory."

"One moment please," the girl on the other end of the phone said.

"Mr. Stewart, this is John Gregory, and I am assuming you have received my letter?"

"Yes, I did, and I must say I was quite shocked at your proposal," Rex said, hoping to lay the groundwork for his conditions.

"My client believes it would be in the best interest of his wife and the child."

"What about my interests?" Rex snapped.

"It is my understanding, Mr. Stewart, you have had very little involvement with the child."

"That is between me and Elizabeth. And, if you expect me to seriously consider your proposal, which I am, I want to be taken care of as well."

"Taken care of, Mr. Stewart?" John Gregory did not like the way this conversation was going.

"Yes, you heard me. I have suffered a great deal since Elizabeth took my son from me and my family, and in order to cope with all of this, I will need to be taken care of."

John Gregory could not believe what he thought this man was suggesting. "You mean you want to be paid in order to meet my client's request?" he asked, feeling his blood pressure rise.

"Yes. I believe I am entitled, as I will have a great deal to contend with on this end, particularly with my mother and the authorities."

"And, how much are we talking about, Mr. Stewart?" John asked, feeling sick now.

"I think twenty thousand US dollars would help."

"And that would be it? You would agree to my client's terms?"

"Yes, but I have a few more conditions."

"Such as?"

"There are three. One: no one is ever to know of the twenty thousand."

"And the others?" John was just disgusted.

"Number two: I do not want my son to be poisoned against me. I do not want your clients to ever say a negative word to him about me."

"And the third condition, Mr. Stewart?"

"That all of the details of this arrangement shall be completely confidential, never to be discussed with anyone, ever."

"I will contact my clients, and I will let you know if they agree."

"Very good."

"Good-bye, Mr. Stewart."

John Gregory slammed down the phone and sat back in his chair, thoroughly disgusted. He had a phone call he did not want to make.

After he conferred with his partners to make sure there would not be any legal repercussions for his clients, and adjusting the wording of this counteroffer, he called

David Williams, who happened to be in his office in New York.

"David, John Gregory here."

"How are you, John?"

"Very well, David. I was calling to let you know I received a telephone call from Rex Stewart."
David sat up to attention in his chair "You did! How did it go? What did he say?"

"I guess it went well. However, amazingly, he has a few conditions of his own."

"He has…conditions?"

"Yes. Basically he has agreed to all of your terms under these conditions." He laid out the rest of the phone conversation for David, slightly embarrassed.

"He wants money!" David railed. "And he wants to walk away scot-free, without any remarks about *his* behavior or any blemishes on *his* reputation? Is he for real?" David was almost shouting into the phone.

"I'm afraid so," John said quietly.

"I need time to absorb this, John."

"Yes, I expect you would."

"What do you think? Do you think we can trust him? Is all of this legal?"

"Yes, if we present it properly."

"Right now, the only thing I agree with is that it is kept confidential, sealed, in fact. I don't ever want anyone to know I had anything to do with this guy."

"I completely understand, David."

"Okay, I will get back with you."

"All right, David." They hung up.

My poor Elizabeth, David thought. *Is this what she has had to deal with? She told me how Rex had abandoned her and Charlie and how she worked during her pregnancy and barely made ends meet. How she had to put up with Kathleen Stewart and Rex's antics. No wonder she was willing to leave the country with Charlie to escape all of them. My poor, brave Elizabeth,* David thought, and that was all he could think about for the next few hours.

David was still in his office, mulling over his conversation with John, when the president of Horton Foods came in.

"Congratulations, I heard you have taken a bride," Steve Horton said.

"Yes, I have, and I have a stepson as well."

"Oh, I see. That would explain why you have been requesting a more permanent position?"

"Yes, Steve, it is time."

"You have always done a great job for us, David, and you have been very loyal to Horton Foods."

"Thank you, Steve."

"We have several major projects coming up that would allow you to make this change, David. Horton Foods would not want you to look elsewhere or to lose you."

"Thank you, Steve. That would be wonderful. We are a little cramped at my family's home, if you get my drift."

"Oh, yes, yes, I do. I will make this happen for you, David. You have earned it."

"Thank you." David stood up, and they shook hands. Steve started to leave his office. Before he reached the door, David quickly said, "Oh, and someplace warm would be preferable."

Steve smiled. "I'll see what I can do." Then he left.

Great! David thought. Now, what to do about Rex Stewart. He decided to stay overnight in New York, needing time to think and too tired to drive back to Vermont. He also wanted to work out the details of Rex Stewart's demands and he wanted to be able to talk to John Gregory with privacy, and that would be hard to do while in the family home in Brattleboro.

He decided he would meet all of Rex's conditions, knowing his promotion was forthcoming. He did not want Elizabeth or Charlie to know what Rex had come up with, and he was not going to hurt them again by telling them. This was between him and Rex now.

He called John Gregory and told him he agreed to Rex's conditions. He told him to revise the documents to reflect that this agreement was between him and Rex and that he did not want Elizabeth and Charlie to ever know about it.

John agreed with his decision and advised him to add a stipulation that Rex could not approach David ever again for additional funds, and that if he did, he would have to repay amounts in full that would include interest and any back child support. He called Rex Stewart to let him know of David's answer and to get other information on how and where to wire his twenty grand. The papers were sent airmail the next day.

CHAPTER TWENTY

Rex was having a late breakfast in Kathleen's kitchen and recovering from a late night out when there was a knock on the door. He heard his mother greet someone and then footsteps as she came closer to the kitchen. He braced himself for another probing conversation with her. She would approach him daily now with questions about Elizabeth and Charlie. She wanted to know where they were and whether or not he had heard from Elizabeth, how Charlie and when was Rex was going to bring him to visit with her.

Rex told no one of his arrangement with David. He could not or he would have a debt that he could never repay. He told himself he would not as he truly wanted Elizabeth and Charlie to have a better life than he could ever give them, even with his mother's help. He had inquired about this David Williams and heard he was a reliable, hard working chap who had never married. If he was true to his word, Elizabeth and Charlie would be better off. It would be the last kind deed he would do for his beautiful Elizabeth. He would let her go.

"Rex a package was just delivered for you and it appears to be from the United States and it looks like it is from a law firm in New York," she said as she squinted to read the envelope.

He rose up quickly from his chair and grabbed the envelope out of her hand saying "Yes, I have been waiting for this".

"What it is about Dear" she asked.

"Oh, it is a small contract for an endorsement I have been hoping for" he said easily as he started for the door.

"I have to get this to the club to have them take a look at it. See you later".

Rex left the house and went straight to the bank. Once in the lobby he took a seat in a quiet area and opened the envelope. He quickly read the document David Williams' attorney had prepared and signed them. He held the Western Union Money Transfer in his hand and stared at it. It read $20,000 U.S. Dollars payable to Rex Stewart. He held it for awhile thinking to himself...*this is the best thing for them. I am doing this for them.* He put the signed documents into the self-addressed, postage paid return envelope provided and he put his copy in his jacket pocket. He stood and walked over to the teller to deposit the money transfer. He kept $100 cash and left the bank. He took a very long walk and ended up on North Beach. He had walked for hours and it was early evening. Most of the beach goers had gone home by now. He found a spot in front of a cluster of sand dunes and sat down. He lit a cigarette and took his copy of the papers from his jacket pocket and held the cigarette to them. He waited for them to catch fire before he dropped them on the sand and watched them burn. No one would ever know.

CHAPTER TWENTY ONE

Steve Horton of Horton Foods was true to his word. Shortly after finalizing the agreement with Rex, Elizabeth and David were moved to Buenos Aires, Argentina. David had purchased, with a little help from Horton Foods, a beautiful home for them not far from the beach. Elizabeth was living the life she had always wanted. She had a maid and cook, and she reveled in running her household, from the gardening to decorating. They entertained quite a bit, as they discovered a lot of other Americans had moved to the growing city of Buenos Aires. David's promotion had been more than they expected, and they flourished. Elizabeth took to buying antiques and fine china and even had her dresses made by a local dressmaker.

Charlie was flourishing too and he had made many friends. He still liked playing with balls, except now he was fascinated with baseballs, which reminded Elizabeth of his father's cricketing and troubled her just a bit. He was learning to speak Spanish easily and was doing well in his preschool. David was a wonderful father for Charlie. He spent every Saturday with him, just the two of them, and they fished and swam and played together, and Charlie started calling him Dad. David's family members were all planning to visit them over the coming months, and they couldn't wait to see them. Abby and Benny were planning to come see them in Argentina very soon and eventually move to the United States permanently too.

Elizabeth and David's love for one another grew more intense every day. With the pressures of her life in South Africa gone and the wonderful life she had now, it was easy. After a year in Buenos Aires, Elizabeth discovered she was pregnant. She knew with David it would be so much better, and she could not wait to bring their child into the world.

One day Elizabeth was looking in her old red suitcase for some photos of David's family, and Benny and Abby. She wanted to frame them and place them in their beautiful living room. She had kept the suitcase as a reminder of home, her travels, and all that she had experienced. Now she used it to store important papers and photographs, at least until she had time to get more organized. As she closed the suitcase after she found the photos she had been looking for, she touched her stomach and smiled. She realized she finally had what she had always wanted, and she planned to enjoy every moment of every day with her beloved David.

Ten years later, Rex Stewart was no longer able to play cricket due to ailing health. His sole focus now, without any guilt, was drinking and womanizing. He had been married six times and was a full-fledged drunk. The Stewart family tried to help him, but he was too far gone. Kathleen died very sad, never understanding what had happened to her favorite son. He drank himself numb every day and died alone and poor, remembering the wife and son he had let slip away.

Elizabeth and David would move from Argentina to Mexico and Puerto Rico, where their second child, a son, was born. They eventually settled in New Canaan, Connecticut where David would commute by train into

New York City to Horton Foods. Rewarded handsomely for his loyalty and his travels on their behalf all over the world he was now a Senior Vice President. They had created a beautiful family, and Elizabeth lived the life she had only dreamed of as a young girl from Boora Rock. David was everything she had hoped for, and he lived up to his promise to her every day of their wonderful life together.

THE END

EPILOGE

Orlando, Florida

It is the year 2010 *as* Charlie sits in his living room with his wife, his two children, his brother and sister and their spouses.

Elizabeth has passed away having lived a full life with David who died the year before. They had all just returned from the funeral and were gathered at Charlie's home. Charlie was very quiet as he remembered bits of his early childhood with Elizabeth, very special memories for him of the two of them.

He got up from his favorite chair and went into his office and opened the closet, it was on the highest shelf. He took it down and carried it to the living room and cleared the coffee table to make a space for it. He set the red suitcase on the table and opened it for the family.

Inside were Elizabeth's pageant and modeling pictures with related newspapers clippings. Many of them never seen by her family. Most noticeable were the many stacks of love letters from David, carefully bound and sorted....